Also by Rachel Harrison
and available from Titan Books

Cackle
Such Sharp Teeth
Black Sheep (Jan 2024)

BAD DOLLS

RACHEL HARRISON

TITAN BOOKS

Bad Dolls
Print edition ISBN: 9781803363936
E-book edition ISBN: 9781803363943

Published by Titan Books
A division of Titan Publishing Group Ltd
144 Southwark Street, London SE1 0UP
www.titanbooks.com

First edition: September 2023
10 9 8 7 6 5 4 3 2 1

A CIP catalogue record for this title is available from
the British Library.

Printed and bound by CPI Group (UK) Ltd,
Croydon, CR0 4YY.

CONTENTS

RACHEL HARRISON

REPLY HAZY, TRY AGAIN

"I NEVER FIND ANYTHING AT THE FLEA," I complained to Maggie as we circumnavigated a couple attempting to get that perfect Instagram shot with the Manhattan Bridge in the background. A crowd had formed on the street, young and trendy, some holding accessories like flowers or balloons, some in fashionable hats. I wondered if they were all waiting their turn for that aspirational snap. I hoped not.

"You have to really dig," Maggie said. "And you have to go regularly. It's like prospecting."

"Okay, Yosemite Sam." I laughed. " 'Prospecting.' Done a lot of prospecting?"

"Yes, can't you tell? I'm pure gold, baby," she said, spinning around and lowering her oversized sunglasses to give me a wink.

Maggie was very glamorous. She had impeccable style;

9

her closet was full of vintage finds. It helped that everything looked good on her. Some people are lucky like that.

Not me.

We got to where the vendors were set up under the bridge and started browsing. Maggie was an intense browser. She liked to stop and examine everything. She was easily compelled. I once made the mistake of going to MoMA with her, and we were there for seven hours. I wasn't a lingerer. It took a lot to catch my interest and a hell of a lot to keep it.

We spent a while thumbing through timeworn postcards and subway maps, observing antique furniture. Then we wandered toward the bins of old action figures and plastic soldiers and displaced Happy Meal toys and limbless baby dolls, all interspersed with matchbooks and baseball cards and buttons and marbles.

It was crap, basically. Just a bunch of crap being sold at a Brooklyn premium.

"Who buys this stuff?" I whispered to Maggie, who was admiring a mustached McNugget in a cowboy hat.

"There's a nostalgia factor," she said. An indirect answer.

I sighed.

"It's good to have things around that bring you joy," she said, and it was as she said this that I spotted the Magic 8 Ball tucked away in a random bin, wedged between a View-Master and a filthy Cabbage Patch Kid.

I reached for it before I understood what I was doing, before I could question what kind of germs occupied its surface. I held it in my hands, turned it around. I couldn't tell how old it was, if it'd been swiped from a Target discount shelf last month or discovered in some grandfather's basement, a precious relic from a childhood long ago.

I gave it a good shake, then read what it had to say, its first words to me.

WITHOUT A DOUBT.

"Oh, cool!" Maggie said. "I always wanted one of those. You should get it."

I wasn't a frivolous spender, but for some reason the 8 Ball seemed like a necessity.

"Yeah," I said. "I should."

When I brought it to the vendor, a man in a backward cap and oversized flannel, he furrowed his brow. "Where'd you find that?"

"That bin. Over there," I said, pointing.

He shrugged, then looked me up and down and said, "Twenty bucks."

It seemed steep, and I almost put it back. But there was something about the weight of it in my hand, how it fit so perfectly in my palm, the way my fingers curled around it, an easy grip. I wanted it, and right as I had this thought, right as the want took root, I looked down at the 8 Ball and now it said, **YES—DEFINITELY.**

I thought it a funny coincidence.

"Fifteen," I told the vendor.

"Okay," he said, nodding.

I'd never haggled before. It was exhilarating.

"Look at you," Maggie said, "Miss I Never Find Anything at the Flea."

I cradled the 8 Ball in my hands. I knew it was illogical to have spent fifteen dollars on something I could have gotten for half that from Amazon, and I typically felt immediate guilt after any impulse purchase, even something as small as gum at the register. I waited for the buyer's remorse to set in, surprised it hadn't already. "Well, I guess this is the exception."

"See, Jordy? When you loosen up and are open to things, you find them, and they find you."

I laughed, charmed by Maggie's faith. "Sure, if you say so. And you know you're the only one who can get away with calling me that."

"Come on, *Jordan*. Let's keep looking. See what treasure awaits."

As we walked, I glanced down at the 8 Ball.

OUTLOOK GOOD, it said.

. . .

Later, Maggie and I sat in Brooklyn Bridge Park, eating sesame bagels with too much cream cheese and drinking iced coffee, savoring our patch of grass and the view of downtown Manhattan. Maggie admired the cameo brooch she had bought at the flea. I took the 8 Ball out of my bag.

YES, it said.

"That will be useful," Maggie said. "You tend to be indecisive."

"Me? No, never," I said. I shook the 8 Ball, which now read, **AS I SEE IT, YES.**

I put it back in my bag.

"You should ask it if Kenny is going to propose."

"Mm," I said, suddenly queasy.

"Apologies," Maggie said, pulling at her collar. "I was just thinking of silly sleepover questions. Does he like me? Is he going to ask me out? Considering you're already past that, well . . ."

I shoved some bagel in my mouth as an excuse not to respond.

"Let's ask it something better," Maggie said, sitting

13

up on her knees. "Why don't we ask it if we'll be friends forever?"

"Really?" I asked.

"Really!" she said. "Please. Let's have a little fun."

"All right." I fished out the 8 Ball and asked, "Will Maggie and I be friends forever?"

I closed my eyes and shook.

I opened my eyes. When I saw what it said, I gasped.

"What?" Maggie leaned over to see. She read it out loud. "'Better not tell you now.' Hmm. How mysterious."

"It's a toy," I said, slipping it into my bag and then zipping the bag shut.

"Yes," Maggie said. "Still . . ."

"Still what?"

She shook her head and then tilted her gaze up, up toward the high noon sun. She was like a sunflower, always seeking the light. She had her summer freckles, abundant across her nose and the tops of her shoulders.

"It's such a beautiful day," she said.

"Yeah," I said. "Beautiful."

• • •

Kenny was in the kitchen, making gnocchi. Making a mess.

"Hey," he said. "How was the flea?"

"You know—the flea," I said, searching the fridge for a seltzer.

"Get anything?"

"No." The lie made a hasty escape. It caught me off guard.

"Oh, well," he said. "Did Maggie?"

"Yeah. She always does. She got a brooch."

He raised an eyebrow. "What's that?"

"A decorative pin," I said. It was what my mother would have called a comma-dumbass sentence. When I was a teenager, I developed a problem with my delivery, my tone. My condescension was out of control. My mother would say, "If it sounds like there's an implied 'comma dumbass' at the end of the sentence, try again."

I opened my mouth, ready to apologize to Kenny for how I'd spoken to him, but part of me resented having to take responsibility for his obliviousness. I changed my mind.

"Ah," he said, unaffected. "Like grandmas wear."

"Exactly."

"Cool," he said. "Dinner will probably be around seven."

"All right. I'm going to go for a run."

He gave a murmur of acknowledgment and returned his concentration to the gnocchi/mess.

I went into the bedroom and changed out of my sundress and into my running gear. I pulled my hair back.

I stretched. I thought about the 8 Ball, where I could put it that Kenny wouldn't find it. I didn't understand why I was so averse to him discovering it, to him touching it, but the idea made me itchy. I thought he might disturb its energy, which I knew was ridiculous. It was unlike me to indulge in such ridiculousness.

Still . . .

I took out the 8 Ball and asked it, "Am I being an idiot?"

CONCENTRATE AND ASK AGAIN, it said.

I huffed. I closed my eyes and gave it some thought. "Is it silly that I don't want Kenny to know about you? That I don't want him to touch you with his gnocchi fingers?"

MY REPLY IS NO, it said.

"Is that more about me or more about Kenny?" As soon as I asked, I knew it was too complex a question for an 8 Ball. I whispered, "Is it him?"

ASK AGAIN LATER.

"Is it me?"

CONCENTRATE AND ASK AGAIN.

"All right," I said. I opened the drawer of my nightstand, moving aside glasses cases and assorted tubes of hand lotion to make space for it.

I was closing the drawer when I saw the 8 Ball now said, **BYE.**

I didn't know that was one of the responses.

"Bye," I said, and then I went for my run.

• • •

Maggie came by my desk the next morning for our usual nine o'clock coffee run. She was wearing a plaid blazer with the brooch on her lapel. Her hair was in a French braid. She wore lipstick, and I noticed because she didn't usually. It was a divine shade of lavender.

"Should we go get Chrissy?" I asked on the way to the elevators.

Occasionally Chrissy, the administrative assistant on Maggie's team, would join us. I liked her. She was fresh out of college and brimming with nervous energy. She always had a story about a hot hookup, about a wild night out, about someone she liked who didn't like her back, about the perils of app dating. She complained about her roommates, about the intricate dramas of unwashed dishes and who paid for toilet paper. She made me feel grateful for my age, for the fact those chaos years were behind me. There are too many hard lessons to be learned in your early twenties. Too much crying outside of H&R Block, in bars, on the subway, in some random hookup's dingy bathroom. Too much crying.

Now that I was thirty, I barely cried. I was delightfully

numb. And I could afford things like Venti Starbucks beverages every morning, an Uber during a downpour, after-work cocktails, meditation apps. Small luxuries that made the days easier.

"She's out today," Maggie said. "Sick day."

"Poor baby."

"Please," Maggie said. "She's probably hungover."

I laughed. "Poor baby."

Maggie shook her head and pressed the elevator button. When the doors closed, she did a funny dance. She liked to dance when we were alone in the elevator. I liked to watch.

"What if there are cameras?" I asked her once.

"Free show," she said, spinning around. "You're welcome."

We got off on the tenth floor and headed to our little corporate-cafeteria Starbucks.

"So, what will it be today?" Maggie asked me. "Back on the chai train? A flat white? A Red Eye? Maybe a matcha?"

She was mocking me because I changed my order every day, constantly waffling about what I wanted while waiting in line. I could never settle on a signature drink.

"Not sure," I said. "Thinking."

"This is why you need the 8 Ball," she said.

"The 8 Ball isn't going to advise me on if I want a hot hazelnut latte or a caramel iced coffee."

"It might," she said. "And it might tell you to just send that email without reading it four thousand times."

"I'm a lawyer," I said. "I'm meticulous."

"Sure," she said, grinning. "So, what'd you do last night?"

I shrugged. "Went for a run. Kenny made gnocchi."

"Did he? Impressive."

I waited for her to tell me that I was lucky. That was what everyone said. I was *so lucky* to have Kenny. I knew they meant well; still, I thought it was mildly insulting at best, dangerous at worst, to say this to someone. Relationships are complicated, and no one could ever really know what goes on from the outside looking in. Why reinforce a reliance, a codependence? Why create this completely unnecessary sense of desperate gratitude? Kenny was great. He was affable and creative and generous, but he was also terribly irresponsible with money and a certified slob. To tell me that I was lucky to be with him dismissed his flaws and my contributions. I did his taxes. I set up his IRA. *So lucky.*

I wasn't certain about much, but I was certain that when it came to relationships, luck was never in play.

At least, fairly certain.

"Make your decision, miss," Maggie said. "You're up."

"You go first."

"Nope," she said. Her flat palm moved up my back and landed between my shoulder blades. She gave me a gentle nudge forward.

My body prickled in the wake of her touch.

I stammered at the counter. "Um . . . sorry . . . I'm sorry. Hazelnut . . . No, sorry. Caramel iced coffee, please. Venti. Light ice. Thank you."

I heard Maggie giggling behind me.

I gave her a look, and she put her hands up in surrender.

We waited for our drinks and then said our goodbyes at the elevator, going to our separate sides of the floor.

I'd been at the company only a few months. Before I started, I worried about the rigid corporate environment, but I ran into Maggie in the bathroom my first week and she invited me to coffee. We became fast friends, a rare fluency between us I'd never quite experienced before. I was excited about her. I told Kenny, all my friends. I'd find any excuse to talk about her.

"Maggie has perfect skin, and she swears by Cetaphil."

"Maggie gave me the recipe for this bomb salad dressing."

"Maggie also loves [insert movie, TV show, musical artist, food, writer, podcast, etc.]."

"As a kid, Maggie almost drowned in Lake Champlain, and she swears Champy saved her."

"I'm glad you made a friend at work," Kenny would say. "We should have her over."

And when he said it, I felt the same way as I did about him with the 8 Ball when I brought it home. I didn't want to let him anywhere near her.

. . .

The following weekend Kenny and I went to Coney Island with his best friend/former college roommate, Sam, and Sam's new girlfriend, Alexa, who had never been.

"It's not how I pictured it would be," she said, her disappointment tangible, contagious.

I felt myself catch it, the threatening tickle of it in the back of my throat. It proliferated swiftly, suffusing me with negativity, cynicism.

When Kenny and I had first started dating, we were constantly taking trips to Coney Island to ride the Cyclone and eat Nathan's and walk up and down the boardwalk, playing new-relationship trivia, where the answer to every question is always prizeworthy, and the prize is you.

Did you ever get injured in gym class growing up? Yes? That is . . . very endearing! You move on to the next round!

A few years in, we already knew pretty much everything there was to know about each other. There was no trivia left, the prize already won. I knew that in third grade Kenny had bruised his coccyx in an unfortunate scooter-board-derby accident. The injury forced him to sleep on his stomach, something he still did to this day. I knew what he was allergic to (shellfish, penicillin). I knew everything he loved (thunderstorms, Dave Grohl, the Yankees, Italian subs, Prospect Park Frisbee, me). I knew his Social Security number.

We were together, game over.

It wasn't that I found him uninteresting. He was well-read and curious. He consumed new information daily and would share it with me over dinner or over text or as we attempted to fall asleep.

"Did you know that aluminum is infinitely recyclable?" he'd said to me the night before as I popped in my retainers.

"No," I responded. "I didn't. That's interesting."

I meant it, but for some reason, it came out with a hint of sarcasm.

That was when I realized if someone you're bored with tells you something compelling, it really doesn't matter what it is. He could have told me that NASA had video footage of little green aliens doing the Macarena on Mars, and I would have yawned.

"Skee-Ball?" Kenny asked me, dragging me out of my

head and back to Luna Park. "Jordan is the Skee-Ball queen."

"It's true," I said, and then proceeded to dominate. I missed the paper tickets, plastic tokens. It was all digital now, your points downloaded onto a card. I felt sorry for younger generations.

When I expressed this to the group, Sam shrugged and said, "It's easier this way."

I looked to Kenny, who nodded in agreement, then to Alexa, who wasn't paying attention. I turned back to Kenny. He smiled at me.

I felt very alone.

That's when I realized if you're looking at someone that you're supposed to love and you feel alone, you have a big problem.

I had a big problem.

"I'll be right back." I handed my arcade card to Kenny and said, "Go crazy."

"Ooh, baby, you treat me so nice," he replied in a funny voice.

I didn't laugh.

I found the nearest bathroom and locked myself in a stall. It smelled terrible, and there was damp toilet paper on the floor, but I found it preferable to the arcade.

"I'm sorry," I whispered to the 8 Ball as I removed it from

my bag. "I apologize for taking you out in these less-than-ideal surroundings, but I need to ask."

I held the 8 Ball in both hands and closed my eyes.

"Am I losing my mind?"

VERY DOUBTFUL, it said.

"Do I love him anymore?"

OUTLOOK NOT SO GOOD.

It was a strange sensation to simultaneously experience the relief of validation and the stark cruelty of the truth.

"Why?" I asked. "Why?"

REPLY HAZY, TRY AGAIN.

I slipped the 8 Ball back into my bag, wrapping it in a scarf.

When I emerged from the bathroom, the stink of it lingered on me. I walked away from the arcade and toward the ocean. I stepped onto the sand, my feet sinking with every step. I watched the waves simmering in the sun. I witnessed the relentless push and pull of the tide. I liked how small and fragile it made me feel, how powerless.

You can't do anything about anything, the ocean seemed to say. *So why bother?*

I wanted to walk into the water. I wanted to march straight into the ocean's mouth and have it swallow me up.

I thought about Maggie almost drowning in Lake Champlain. I thought about Champy, the American Loch

Ness Monster. I thought about how sweet it was, her faith in folklore. The first time we had gone for drinks after work, she told me she wanted to take a weekend trip to the Pine Barrens to search for the Jersey Devil.

"Why?" I asked her.

She smiled against the rim of her coupe, a gin gimlet swirling below, anxious to meet her lips.

"Because," she said. "Because I like to meet other strange creatures. Good to know I'm not alone."

• • •

On the train back from Coney Island, Kenny held my hand. It wasn't typical behavior, but Sam had his arm around Alexa, so perhaps he felt obligated.

The four of us went to dinner at a restaurant near Sam's apartment in Ditmas Park, and afterward we walked around admiring the neighborhood houses.

"We should live here," Kenny said to me. "Get one of these. Chill on the porch."

"Sure," I said. "Definitely."

"I like this area," he said.

I wondered if he was serious, if he actually thought we could afford one of the massive Victorians. I wondered what it was like to be such an idealist. I wanted a cigarette.

"Is it too far to walk?" he asked me. "To walk home?"

"No," I said. "Probably about forty-five minutes."

"Cool. Down to walk?"

"Yep." I reached into my bag and felt for the 8 Ball. I wondered what it said now, if anything.

My phone vibrated against the back of my hand. I took it out. I had a text from Maggie.

Brunch tomorrow?

Yes, please, I thought. *I need to tell you about Coney Island. I need to ask if you miss the paper arcade tickets like I do, if you, too, appreciated the tangible victory, if you're also sad about the digitization of the world. I need to know if you understand because I really think you will.*

But I didn't say any of that. I didn't respond at all.

I need, I need, I need.

I clutched the 8 Ball.

. . .

I faked sick on Monday. I lied to Kenny, to my manager.

"Migraine," I told them.

To Maggie, I said nothing.

I sat alone in my apartment, curtains drawn, chewing on my nails and hovering over the 8 Ball.

26

"Should I break up with Kenny?"

YES.

"Fuck," I said. "When?"

DON'T COUNT ON IT.

"What does that mean?"

JORDAN.

I blinked. I shook it again.

JORDAN.

My mouth went dry, my eyes; then my body floated away.

It was my name. In a neat white font. On the blue triangle, in the round window. My name.

And then . . . the triangle began to move. All on its own. It rolled backward to reveal a new message.

COME ON.

And again.

YOU KNOW.

Again.

YOU ALREADY KNOW.

ALL THIS.

YOU'VE KNOWN.

FOR A WHILE.

The ball slid from my sweat-slick hands, down to the floor with a *thunk*. At first, I was too terrified to lean over to pick it up. But after a few minutes passed, I was too scared not to. I didn't want to upset it. I reached with trembling fingers.

OW, it said.

Ow.

. . .

"Are you feeling better?" Kenny asked me when he got home from work.

"No," I said, which was technically true.

"Oh," he said, haunting the doorway. "Do you need anything?"

"Don't think so," I said, collapsing back onto my pillow. "Trying to sleep it off."

"Okay. Well, if you need anything, just holler."

"Yep."

When I heard the door latch, I returned to what I was doing—using my phone as a flashlight inside my fortress of sheets, interrogating the 8 Ball.

"Will I be any happier if I leave him?" I asked, for the tenth time.

CANNOT PREDICT NOW, it answered for the tenth time.

"Really?" I asked it. "Or do you just not want to tell me?"

ENOUGH ALREADY, it replied.

I sighed. "What good are you if you can't give me specific instructions or guarantee my eternal happiness?"

HEY NOW, it said.

"I was kidding."

EVEN SO.

I didn't have to shake it anymore. It responded all on its own, the triangle shifting inside the mysterious blue liquid.

"I'm sorry," I mumbled, putting it back in my nightstand drawer.

I turned over and swaddled myself in the sheets. I tried to recall when exactly I had started being unhappy. When I had fallen out of love with Kenny. I couldn't pinpoint a moment.

I tried to remember when I first knew that I loved Kenny and why. But I couldn't identify that either. I began to question whether I had ever loved him, or if I was just doing what I thought I was supposed to be doing.

At twenty-six, meet someone at the birthday party of mutual friend. Flirt over a pitcher of cheap beer. Exchange numbers. Talk for a week over text, then go out to dinner. Get along. Have decent sex. Continue hanging out. Decide to move in together. The city is so expensive. Why not? We're old enough. Why not?

"Isn't it so great to find someone to be with? To share a life with?" my old boss asked me when I took the day off to move. When I came back to the office the following Monday, I found a card on my desk signed by all my coworkers congratulating me on my new place. They collectively bought me a housewarming gift, a small ficus. It was a sweet gesture, I guess, but a real pain to transport on the train.

It was as I presented this ficus to Kenny that I decided I wanted a new job, that I didn't want to go back to that office. I was embarrassed. I didn't quite know why. It took me a while to find a new position, and by then, I'd sort of forgotten about the ficus. It had died.

I retrieved the 8 Ball from my drawer. I felt untethered, uncertain that I'd ever decided anything for myself. I was infamously meticulous, agonizing endlessly over logistics. It was always about what made sense, about meeting expectations, perceived success. Never about what would make me happy, what I desired. Want was a nonfactor.

Kenny and I had been together for four years, so it wasn't uncommon for us to get asked when we planned on getting married. My reaction was instant nausea, but also, I would think, *Probably next fall.*

Why had I always been so content to ignore my own discontentment?

Why now this crisis of faith?

"Is it you?" I asked the 8 Ball.

MY REPLY IS NO.

"Is it me?"

VERY DOUBTFUL.

I took a breath. Why now this want?

"Is it her?"

I didn't need to look to know the answer.

. . .

In an act of true cowardice, I arranged to work from home for the rest of the week, citing cluster headaches.

Are you all right? Miss you at the office, Maggie texted me.

Headaches, I replied, a heat rising in my cheeks. Get them this time of year. Usually last a few days.

A few days? she said. How can I survive here without you?

I fumbled for the 8 Ball.

"Is Maggie into me?" I asked.

NICE TRY.

In the hot haze of frustration, I spat, "You're fucking useless!" and shoved it away.

I watched in horror as it slowly rolled itself back toward me. It stopped just shy of my fingertips, its murky eye faceup, glaring at me. The blue triangle floated into view, the lettering on it now red instead of white.

BE CAREFUL, it said.

I reached for it, ready to shut it in my drawer and pretend it didn't exist. But then I saw it said, **DON'T YOU DARE.**

I pulled my hand away and my knees to my chest, rocking back and forth, back and forth, staring at it.

APOLOGIZE AND ASK AGAIN.

"I'm . . . I'm sorry," I said, a pathetic quaver warping my voice. "Um . . . is Maggie into me?"

CANNOT PREDICT NOW. The letters were white again.

"Okay," I squeaked. "Thank you."

ASK AGAIN LATER.

I didn't want to, but I knew I would.

. . .

Kenny went out to dinner with his coworkers that Thursday, so I took a walk to pick up some pho for myself, forcing myself out of the apartment and away from the 8 Ball, which I'd been obsessively checking for forty-eight hours straight. Sneaking it into the bathroom in the middle of the night while Kenny was asleep, kneeling on the wet floor and just holding it, waiting for it to tell me something, anything. It wasn't good. It wasn't healthy. I was scaring myself. I felt out of control.

I left early and wandered a bit. I studied everyone I passed. A mother in a business-casual wrap dress and loafers scrolling on her phone as her son scootered beside her, his helmet comically large. A student with a hot pink backpack slung over her shoulder, drinking a Grande Frappuccino with whip, the Bose noise-canceling headphones that I deemed too expensive hanging around her neck like jewelry. A man in unironic corduroy overalls smoking a cigarette and staring right at me.

Two women, their arms around each other. One in a satin jumpsuit that looked like chic pajamas, the other in high-waisted jeans and a white ribbed tank. One wearing makeup, the other none. One with a septum piercing and tattoo sleeve; the other might have had piercings and tattoos but they were secrets.

They were obviously together. They moved in sync as if they were a single entity with four legs. They laughed, and I clung to the rhythm of their laughter, wanting to commit it to memory so I could access it again, fearing I might never experience it for myself.

I picked up my soup and brought it home. I ate it on the living room floor, resisting the temptation of the 8 Ball in the other room. I could hear it rolling itself around in my drawer, knocking against the wood, rattling my things. I watched a documentary about an infamous art heist to distract myself, volume up high.

I thought it was a shame that the paintings had never been found but admired the audacity of the thieves. I pictured a Rembrandt collecting dust in someone's basement.

I pictured my own heart.

. . .

I relented.

"When?" I asked the 8 Ball as I sat on the bathroom floor underneath the towel rack, my forehead against the wall, a used towel draped over me like a damp veil. It was four o'clock in the morning.

TONIGHT, it said.

"Really? Tonight?"

YES.

So, after Kenny left for work, I packed a suitcase and booked a hotel.

The room was expensive, but I figured I would want to be alone after I did it. *If* I did it.

. . .

I could recognize Kenny's footsteps coming down the hall, his particular cadence.

I felt a leap of regret, but my suitcase was already packed, and I had no backup excuse, no way of explaining it away.

34

I realized I should have just left. I shouldn't have waited for him to come home. Was it really noble to do it in person? Was there anything noble about what was about to go down?

He opened the door.

"Hey," he said. "You're up! Are you feeling better?"

Was the decision rash? Was I being too impulsive?

Was it the influence of the 8 Ball?

"Not really," I said. "I have to talk to you about something."

"Okay," he said. "Mind if I shower first? It's humid out there. I'm sweating like a pig."

"Sure," I said. "Actually, no. It can't wait."

He set his keys down on the counter. "What is it?"

It was so surreal. It was years of cohabitation, of alternating family holidays, of watching the same TV shows at the same time, of discovering new recipes and sharing bottles of wine. As much as I hated to admit it, my old boss had been right. Kenny and I had shared a life. We had built a life, and it was ours. It was mine.

And I was about to incinerate it because of an office crush.

Except it wasn't just an office crush.

I wished it was.

I really wished it was.

I mustered up some courage and struck the match.

. . .

Once I was able to admit to myself that I felt for her, I was able to understand how *much* I felt for her. The thoughts I'd been resisting poured through, a great dam breaking. I thought about her scent, rose and cedarwood, and coffee, usually. Her hands soft, slight, her nails cut short. Her skin perfect, dewy. Her eyebrows untamed. Her lashes thick, with a natural curl. Her hair wavy, the color of rich chocolate. Her long regal neck.

I thought about her fashion sense, about the grace of her movements. She had immaculate posture from years of dance. She was also an equestrian. She had gone to Yale. She laughed about it.

One time we went to a post-work yoga class, and afterward she changed into her Yale sweatshirt and a pair of loose jeans.

I pictured her wearing that, descending the steps of the Astor Place subway station, the passing uptown train blowing back her hair. I pictured a tiny brass key twisting inside a tiny brass lock. Was that the moment? Was that when it had all started? Or had it started the moment I first saw her in the office bathroom, her reflection materializing next to mine like some kind of magic? Our eyes met in the mirror, and *poof*. A forever change.

· · ·

I soaked in the tub of my hotel room until I pruned, until the only things I felt were abstract and I could pretend I was in a dream.

I wrapped myself in a towel and sprawled across the king-sized bed, my wet hair dripping onto the pillows. I sipped a nip of gin from the minibar. I ate cold room service French fries. I kept the 8 Ball in sight. I ignored the constant buzzing of my phone, likely Kenny or the mutual friends he'd already informed about our breakup.

He had seemed upset, though I wouldn't have said devastated.

"If that's how you feel," he'd said.

"I still love you. It's just, I don't think we're each other's person, you know?"

I hated myself for saying it, but I knew he would respond to it. I knew he could regurgitate this detail on future dates, to future girlfriends. To a future wife. They'd lap it up, I thought. He'd be fine. I knew he would be fine. He was now an eligible young bachelor in New York City. His IRA already set up.

"I'll miss you," he'd told me.

"I'll miss you, too," I'd said. I was afraid I meant it.

"Did I make a mistake?" I asked the 8 Ball.

REPLY HAZY, TRY AGAIN.

I let it roll away from me.

I turned over onto my back and stared at the ceiling.

I thought about the color of Maggie's hair in sunlight.

. . .

The next morning, I watched the sun rise over the ever-changing skyline of downtown Brooklyn. I counted the distant cranes. I yawned, then reached for the 8 Ball before anything else. Before checking my phone. Before brushing my teeth. Before peeing.

"Are you on my side?" I asked it.

MOST LIKELY.

"Please. Tell me the truth."

YOU MAY RELY ON IT.

"I need you."

I KNOW.

I thought back to when I had found it at the flea two weeks prior. I thought about whether I was grateful that I'd found it, whether I would have ever taken action if I hadn't. I thought about how, that day, Maggie had told me I was indecisive. I'd always known I was, but I hadn't understood then what I did now: that it was all born of fear. I'd lived my whole life afraid, oblivious to my own trepidation. I wondered if the problem was universal, or if I was particularly weak.

I thought about how Maggie had brought up Kenny proposing.

"Was she jealous?" I asked the 8 Ball.

BETTER NOT TELL YOU NOW.

"That's what you said. When we asked you if we'd be friends forever, you said the same thing."

At first, I felt hopeful. Maybe it meant we wouldn't be friends because we'd be something more. But then I realized it could just as easily have meant that we weren't friends because I had confessed romantic feelings for her that were unreciprocated. Unwelcome.

I wasn't brave enough for any of it.

I considered going back to bed, retreating into sleep, but then my phone started to ring.

It was Kenny.

"Should I answer it?" I asked the 8 Ball.

OH, MY GOD, it said. Then, **I'M EXHAUSTED.**

"Sorry. I'm sorry."

I didn't pick up.

Instead, I rolled to the edge of the mattress and surrendered to gravity, let it do the hard work of getting me out of bed.

I started packing, then decided I wasn't ready to check out. I extended my stay another night.

I foraged in my suitcase for an acceptable outfit. I wanted to feel good in public, to look better than I felt. I put on a pair of wide-legged jeans and a sleeveless blouse. I had brought only the one pair of shoes. Classic Keds, the soles worn hazardously smooth.

"You want to come?" I asked the 8 Ball.

I didn't know where I was going yet, but I knew I had to go somewhere. I couldn't stay in the hotel, staring at the walls and courting a Jack-from-*The Shining* mental state.

SURE, the 8 Ball said.

I put it in my bag, along with my wallet and my phone, now in airplane mode to stop its constant buzzing.

I left the hotel and went around the corner to the snobby coffee shop where they served French pastries and exceptional espresso drinks. I got myself an almond croissant, a blueberry scone, and a large latte. I thought I would sit outside, where there were tables set up on the sidewalk, but decided there was too much traffic. I wanted somewhere more scenic.

I walked in a daze until I was tripping over cobblestones in Dumbo. The flea was there only on Sundays; on Saturdays it was someplace else. Maybe Williamsburg or Industry City. Fine by me, I wasn't there for the flea.

I bought flowers from a bodega and positioned myself under the Manhattan Bridge.

"Would you mind taking my picture?" I asked a stranger, who I suspected was also waiting for a photo op. "I can take yours, too."

They nodded with such enthusiasm that I regretted asking, because I worried that I would disappoint with my lackluster photography skills.

I let them go first.

When it was my turn, I tried not to be self-conscious. I tried to let go of all judgment, of everything and everyone around me, of myself. I tried to just exist for a moment in the moment. Free of expectation. Free of analysis.

I smiled.

. . .

I sat near the carousel picking at my croissant. I watched the hundred-year-old wooden horses gallop around in the same circle. I wondered if they were bored. *They must be*, I thought. *Poor things.*

I watched boats amble along the East River. I watched the slow drift of clouds.

I examined the picture of myself under the Manhattan Bridge. I zoomed in on my face. I didn't look happy, but I did look pretty. There was, miraculously, no one else in the shot. I looked alone in the world, which was great for the photo but not for reality.

"Should I call Maggie?" I asked the 8 Ball.

YES—DEFINITELY.

So I did.

"Hello, hello," she said. "Please tell me those pesky headaches are gone."

"They are," I said with a twinge of guilt for lying.

"Good. What are you up to this weekend?"

"Actually, I . . . I . . . uh . . . Kenny and I broke up last night."

"Wait. What? Seriously? Are you okay?"

"Yeah, I'm fine," I said. "I'm at Jane's Carousel eating carbs. I'm fine."

"Are you sure, Jordy? Do you want me to come?"

"If you want," I said, attempting to be casual.

"I'm there," she said. "Let me throw on some clothes and I'll grab a car."

"No rush," I said. "I'm really fine."

"I believe you," she said. "Still . . ."

We exchanged quick goodbyes and hung up.

I wiped my hands on my jeans and took out the 8 Ball. In my head, I ran through all the questions I wanted to ask about the future, distant and not so distant. I wanted to ask what was about to happen. I wanted to ask what I should do.

Should I tell Maggie how I felt about her? Should I wait?

Should I keep it to myself, carry the secret around hoping it would eventually disappear?

Was I ready to jump into another relationship?

Did any of it matter? Even if Maggie did return my feelings, who could say how long it would all last? Maybe eventually I would feel indifferent about her, the way I did with Kenny.

Was I searching for happiness in the wrong places? Seeking it in other people instead of turning my gaze inward?

I swiped my thumb over the bold black-and-white number. *Why eight?* I wondered.

Maybe it wasn't about the number; maybe it was the symbol. Infinity. Maybe because there were infinite questions to ask, maybe because wonder was limitless. There were so many variables, so many unknowns.

I could sit with the 8 Ball forever, asking and asking but never getting any closer to enlightenment. Never learning a damn thing.

It could never tell me what I needed to know. It could never give me any comfort, any guarantees, any confidence, any courage. It could only raise more questions, loop me into an endless cycle of need, questions begetting more questions.

I thought about throwing the 8 Ball into the river, winding my arm like a pitcher and catapulting it into the murky waters, among Mafia skeletons and lost treasure and trash.

But I couldn't bring myself to do it.

I looked up and saw Maggie coming toward me, wearing her Yale sweatshirt, khakis, and Converses, her hair in low pigtails.

I asked the 8 Ball a silent question, promising it would be my last.

It answered, **SIGNS POINT TO YES.**

BACHELORETTE

IF I'D BEEN TOLD IN ADVANCE about the blood sacrifice, I would have made up an excuse not to attend the bachelorette party. I wasn't too enthused about going in the first place. I resented group activities, especially ones where everyone else involved seemed delighted to participate. It made me wonder if I was just a miserly curmudgeon for not wanting to shell out my hard-earned income on someone else's idea of a good time. Did no one else find it all ridiculous? The engagement party and the bridal shower and the bachelorette weekend and the wedding week.

"I'm going to end up dropping five K on someone else's wedding," I complained to my mother over the phone as I packed my suitcase in advance of Hailey's Whimsical Woodland Weekend. "And why does everything have to have a theme now?"

"Not like you need the money for your own wedding," my mother said.

"Well," I said, contemplating a pair of shorts, "that's your fault, not mine. You raised me to be fiercely independent."

"Natalie."

"I should send you the link to her registry. It's unconscionable. They've lived together in that house for two years. They don't *need* anything. They've got a frog statue on the registry. Ceramic frogs sitting on a log. I believe they're fishing. It's a hundred and fifty dollars. For fucking frogs."

"Language," my mother said. "Why are you so worked up about this?"

I folded the shorts and placed them in my suitcase, then collapsed onto my bed. "Why do we, as a society, reward people for getting married?"

"It's a celebration," my mother said. "We need to celebrate things in life. Otherwise . . ."

Her voice trailed off. I heard her sip what I knew was Diet Dr Pepper in a porcelain teacup. She liked things the way she liked them and never apologized for it, which was good and fine, but somehow it was a mystery to her how and why I turned out the way I did.

"Why don't we celebrate other accomplishments?" I asked. "Why all the hoopla over forsaken freedom?"

"Natalie. This isn't about you and your burning bra. This is about Hailey. This is for Hailey."

My mother was right. Hailey was my oldest friend. We'd grown up together. Countless sleepovers watching dumb comedies and staying up past midnight, whispering secrets. Slipping notes into each other's lockers, cutting class together. Swapping clothes and boys. We'd gossip about who was a good kisser, who used too much tongue. When we got our licenses, we'd drive around town for hours, listening to angsty emo rock and contemplating the future.

Now the future was here, and she was getting married to someone I barely knew. Mike seemed fine. In my eyes no one would ever be worthy; Hailey was the sweetest and most fun person I'd ever met. I had other friends, friends whom I loved and was close to, but they weren't special to me the way that Hailey was. When you're young with someone, when you share those formative years, the bond is specific and sincere.

"Nat?"

"I have to finish packing," I said, my voice weirdly high. "Thanks for listening to me vent."

"Anytime. Love you."

"Love you, too." When I hung up, I noticed I had a text from Hailey.

Can't wait to see you this weekend!! it read. Miss you so much!

I plugged my phone in, and as it charged, I scrolled through old photos.

The two of us at our eighth-grade graduation, our smiles metallic, our dresses glittery, butterfly clips in our hair.

The two of us at sixteen sitting on the curb outside the mall, wearing tank tops and too much eyeliner, eating from the same bag of Swedish Fish.

A selfie of us in Hailey's car, our eyebrows plucked thin, our lips pouty, the picture taken at a Myspace angle.

After a while, looking at the pictures stopped being fun and started to be painful. It was an icky feeling, a squirming in my chest. I patted away a few rogue tears and continued packing, busying myself in an attempt to escape the emotion.

The emotion that was, in retrospect, a warning.

• • •

I admired the constellations on the ceiling of Grand Central while sipping tepid coffee and eating a cranberry muffin, killing time before my train departed. Brianna would be picking me up from the station in Cold Spring. The house itself wasn't in Cold Spring, and I didn't know where it was

48

exactly, because I couldn't be bothered to read Brianna's extensive emails. She was Hailey's maid of honor, and she approached each task with such intensity you'd have thought she was defusing a bomb. At the bottom of every email she would write, in bold, Please get back to me by 4:30 PM today at the latest. I would often purposely wait until a few minutes past her deadline to spite her, but then she began emailing me reminders, so I surrendered my passive-aggressive game.

Hailey had met Brianna in college, and they stayed close postgraduation. They had a lot in common, lived within walking distance, had regular wine nights and gym dates, vacationed together. Still, whenever I was around, Brianna was hostile toward me—as if I was a threat to their friendship. She liked to assert her position as *the* best friend. I thought her attachment to Hailey a little strange, verging on obsessive. But at the same time, I absolutely did not want to be the one negotiating necklines of bridesmaid's dresses and ordering custom aprons as shower favors. I was grateful that she was doing all the heavy lifting, and all I had to do was show up.

Though even showing up felt like a lot for me.

I headed toward the train, realizing if I continued to dawdle, I might miss it. My phone buzzed with a text from

Brianna asking if I would be arriving on schedule. While distracted, responding with a simple yep, I accidentally bumped shoulders with a man in a business suit.

"Fucking bitch," he spat.

Stellar way to start the weekend, I thought, stepping onto the train just as the doors closed behind me.

I found a seat, and as I watched New York City blur into the Hudson Valley, I tried to will away my cynicism. Though most of the bridesmaids were, like Brianna, Hailey's friends from college whom I didn't know that well because I'd gone away to school while Hailey stayed in Jersey, there was one other exception. Hailey's sister-in-law-to-be, Jaqueline. Jacqueline wasn't part of the friend group either. She was a few years older than the rest of us and lived in Philly with her wife and their two kids. I'd met her only once before, at the bridal shower, but I liked her vibe. We sat next to each other while Hailey opened her gifts, and whispered our predictions.

"A crossbow," Jaqueline deadpanned when Hailey held up a petite box tied with a frilly pink ribbon, which ended up containing a crystal soap dish.

"A burner phone," I'd said before Hailey flung back some tissue paper and pulled out a cake stand.

Maybe the bachelorette weekend wouldn't be so bad. At least it wasn't a bar crawl wearing penis crowns. I had initially suggested a night out in the city, because then I wouldn't have to be inconvenienced by travel. I envisioned something fun and classy. Beauty & Essex, followed by a speakeasy like Please Don't Tell. Brunch at Balthazar the next morning. But I wasn't specific in my email, and as soon as I sent it, I worried that my NYC Bachelorette? proposal could easily result in a Times Square nightmare, navigating around the Broadway crowds, bumping elbows with Hoboken bros. No, thank you.

Hailey wants to do something more low-key, Brianna replied all of two minutes later. I'm looking into renting us this dreamy Airbnb in NY. She wants to go for more of a woodland theme. Will keep you posted! Xo, Bri.

Bri was waiting for me when I stepped off the train, standing beside her neon green Ford Fiesta, waving violently. She was smiling so widely her lips curled over her unnervingly white teeth.

I gave her a quick salute. "Hey there."

"Hey, you!" she said. She popped the trunk, and when I went to put my suitcase inside, I noticed a small wooden box and some rope, but didn't think much of it. "Wait till you see the place. You're going to die!"

"Great," I said, climbing into the passenger seat. Her car smelled like a piña colada.

"The house was built in 1790. It's so, so cute," she said. "Gum?"

I held out my palm and she tapped a piece into it. It was blue and tasted like cotton candy.

"It's been renovated, obviously. Has all the amenities."

"No outhouse?"

"God, no," she said. "We will have to share rooms. I have you in with Jacqueline."

I wasn't thrilled about having to bunk with someone like it was summer camp, especially since I had paid five hundred dollars for the two nights, but at least I was with Jacqueline.

"So, I emailed you the itinerary, but I didn't hear back, so I'll just tell you now really quick, so you know what the plan is," she said.

I fought the urge to immediately tune her out.

"Okay," I said. "Let's hear it."

"When we get back, we'll kick it off with a champagne happy hour. I've got all the stuff for a champagne-bar situation. We'll toast and mix champagne cocktails. Then we're going to dinner in town tonight. I've got reservations at, like, a pub-type place. Burgers and stuff. After, we'll come back here, movie night. Popcorn, candy, et cetera. Hailey wants to watch *Bridesmaids*."

"Appropriate choice," I said.

"Tomorrow morning I've got a yoga instructor coming. We're going to do outdoor yoga. The yoga is sixty, by the way," she said. "We're all pitching in for Hailey, obviously."

"Obviously," I said through clenched teeth.

"After yoga, I got us stuff to make brunch. I'll cook. I'm happy to cook. Then I've got this girl coming in who does, like, catering and flowers and setup and everything. Did you get my email about that?"

"Yep." I did but I'd suppressed it. It was another two hundred and fifty dollars.

"Did you look at her Instagram? So amazing, right?"

"Yeah, amazing." I hadn't looked.

"Then drinks and music, and I got this bachelorette party game. It's like Cards Against Humanity, kind of, but for bachelorette parties. And yeah! I've got some really, *really* special plans for tomorrow night. All fun stuff Hailey will love."

"Cool. So tonight, dinner and a movie. Tomorrow night, general shenanigans."

"Yes. Sunday morning bagels. Then I'll take you back to the station. How's that sound?"

"It sounds super fun," I said, trying out some zest. "Thank you for organizing all of this. I appreciate it."

"Anything for my Hailey."

My Hailey. I wondered if she thought I was dumb. I wondered if she thought it bothered me.

It didn't. Because I knew that Hailey and I were more than friends. We were an amalgam of pinkie promises and inside jokes and hundreds of phone calls and shared lip balms and deep confessions. We had survived puberty together. I could list every crush she'd ever had, every person she'd ever kissed. I was there when her parents split up and I held her as she cried. I knew the taste of her tears. I knew the pitch of her laugh; it lived in me.

We were sisters.

So Bri could get fucked.

. . .

The house was fine. Old, made of stone, with a wraparound porch that looked like a recent addition. It was set back in the woods. I worried about ticks.

"Isn't it *so* cute?" Brianna asked me as we pulled up, and again as I got my suitcase out of the trunk.

I pointed to the wooden box, which I saw had some engraving on it. "Do you need this?"

She slammed the trunk shut, ignoring my question. "What do you think of the house, Nat?"

"Cute," I said. "So cute."

"Like out of a fairy tale or something," she said, leading me up the porch steps. "So perfect for the theme."

Ah, yes, I thought. *The* theme.

Brianna opened the front door, and I experienced the resurgence of the squirmy ickiness I had felt when I was packing. It was like there was a creature thrashing around in my chest. A shark. Something wild and hungry and totally alone. Something dangerous.

"Hello, hello!" Brianna sang.

Inside, the house looked as I had expected it to. Low ceilings, hardwood, a stone fireplace, a remodeled kitchen with all-new appliances and a big marble island. It was very catalog. Very Instagram-able.

Hailey was sitting on the living room floor, her hands splayed on the coffee table, Chiara painting her nails. Shelby was perched behind Chiara, watching from the couch. Chiara and Shelby were never far from each other. They were best friends and former dorm mates, while Hailey and Brianna had shared a room across the hall. Junior year, the four of them had gotten a suite.

"Look at you in that leather jacket," Hailey said, swiveling her head toward me but keeping her body perfectly still as to not disturb the manicure.

"It's too warm out but I had to wear it. How else would people know I'm cool?"

"Oh, they'd know," she said.

"Hi, Natalie," Shelby chirped from the couch. She was five foot nothing, a former ballerina who now taught dance to children and had a lifestyle blog. She was incredibly blond and had thick, straight bangs. She looked so good with bangs, I wanted to sue.

Chiara did not look up from her careful work. She was an aesthetician employed at a high-end spa in Mendham, where all the rich housewives went to maintain their youth. She was always in designer clothes. Today she wore a Fendi print top paired with deliberately ripped jeans.

"Hey, Nat," she said.

"Hey, hey," I said, waving.

"I'll show you your room and then we can start the festivities," Brianna said, taking my suitcase and ushering me down the hall.

Jacqueline was already in the room, lying on one of the beds and FaceTiming with her kids. I heard their sweet little voices saying, "Mommy! Mommy, look!"

"That's great," Jacqueline said, giving me a nod. She mouthed, *Sorry.*

I gave her a "don't worry about it" shake of the head.

"Champagne in five?" Brianna asked Jacqueline.

"Sure," Jacqueline said. "Be right there."

"Where's the bathroom?" I asked Bri.

She pointed to the door across the hall.

"Thanks," I said. "I'm just going to wash up. I'll be out in a few."

Brianna gave me a look that I couldn't decode.

"What?" I asked after a few seconds of her ambiguous stare.

"Just remember not to mention Dana. We're all really disappointed she couldn't come."

Dana was Hailey's sixth bridesmaid, another college friend. Brianna had called me earlier that week to inform me that Dana could no longer make the bachelorette, her tone so somber I initially thought someone had died.

"She can't make it," Brianna had repeated. "Hailey's devastated."

"Is Dana okay?" I asked.

There was a long pause. Finally, Bri had huffed and said, "Her mother fell and broke her jaw."

"Jesus," I said. "Is her mom all right?"

"She'll be fine. I'm just trying to figure out how to salvage the weekend the best I can."

"I'm sure Hailey understands. We'll still have a good time."

"Hopefully," Brianna had said. "I just wanted to let you know because I don't want it to come up this weekend. No mention of Dana."

It seemed extreme, but I'd agreed because it was easier that way.

I gave Brianna a thumbs-up and circled her to get to the bathroom. I locked the door behind me and savored my two minutes of seclusion. When I opened the door, there was Jacqueline. She smiled at me and gave me a hug.

"Good to see you, comrade," she said.

"You, too."

"Shall we go anesthetize ourselves?"

"Please."

Brianna had created an elaborate, adorable setup in mere minutes. The kitchen island was decorated with succulents in small metal pails. There were polka-dot bowls filled with pretzels and cocktail nuts. There were many, many bottles of champagne. There were plastic champagne flutes, a variety of liquors and juices and syrups, laminated cards with types of cocktails on the front and recipes on the back. There was a wooden sign that read *Bachelorette Weekend* in loopy script.

"Let's make some cocktails and have a toast!" Brianna shouted over the music, a playlist I'm sure she had carefully curated. It kicked off with "Lady Marmalade."

Brianna popped the first bottle and everyone whooped and giggled. I went ahead and started mixing myself a drink without referencing any of the recipe cards, something that Brianna noted and clearly did not appreciate.

"The cocktails on the cards are tried-and-true," she said.

"Going off book?" Hailey asked.

"Yep," I said, pouring a splash of Cointreau in my flute. "What are you gonna go for?"

"Hmm," she said. She picked up a bottle of Chambord. "Remember when we used to sneak this from the liquor cabinet when my mom was out?"

"We'd mix it with orange juice."

"Was it good? I forget."

"No idea," I said. "What did we know then?"

"What do we know now?" she asked, pouring some into a flute and then reaching for the OJ.

"You're doing it?" I asked her.

"I'm doing it," she said. "Throwback."

"Then I'll have one, too."

I looked up just in time to catch Brianna's eye. She was wrathful.

She pulled it together to give a toast. "Let's raise our glasses to our bride, Hailey, my best friend in the whole world. I love you, Hailey! And I'm so excited for this weekend, for the surprises to come, and to celebrate *you*. And I'm just so happy you all are here. Now let's show our girl a good time! Cheers, bitches!"

"Cheers!" everyone said, tapping our plastic flutes together.

"Not bad," Hailey said, sipping the drink from our reckless teen past.

"Nahh, dude, too sweet," I said, spitting it back into my flute.

"That's why we use the cards," Brianna said.

"You're right, you're right," Hailey said, beginning to browse through them.

Brianna gave me a smug look. I waited for her to turn away and then covertly poured the rest of my drink into a conveniently located houseplant.

After we all finished our drinks, we were instructed to go back to our rooms to get changed for dinner.

"I'm just wearing this," Jacqueline said through a yawn. "Can't be bothered."

"No judgment from me," I said. "I'm not changing because I'm a conformist. I'm changing because I was on public transportation."

"Mm," she said. "Fair enough."

I was tempted to make a snarky comment about Bri but

held back. I didn't want to be petty. Not openly anyway. Not in front of Jacqueline, whom I genuinely liked and whom I wanted to like me. Cattiness was unbecoming and I didn't want to alienate an ally. So I held my tongue.

I changed clothes. Then Jacqueline and I joined the rest of the group in the living room, where Chiara was fixing Shelby's eyeliner and Hailey sat on the floor, holding her phone in one hand and a giant curling iron in the other.

I plopped down next to her. She smelled wonderfully familiar. She'd worn the same perfume since seventh grade: Curious by Britney Spears.

"Let me do your hair," she said. "You look so pretty with curls."

"I don't look pretty now?"

She rolled her eyes.

"Fine, fine," I said, turning around and removing my scrunchie.

I felt the gentle pull of her hands in my hair and closed my eyes. It was like we were back at one of our sleepovers, lounging around and getting all dolled up for no reason. Maybe later we'd make prank calls.

"Hailey, can you come here for a sec?" Bri hollered from somewhere. "I need help picking an outfit."

"I can finish her up, Hail," Chiara said. "You can go."

"Really? Cool, thanks! B-R-B."

I almost said something about her abandoning me, but I let it go.

Chiara yanked my hair back. "Nat, your ends are so dry. You need a trim."

"Yeah, I know." That would have been enough to annoy me, but then . . . "Ow, fuck! Did you just burn me?"

"Oh, sorry, hon! My bad."

She didn't sound sorry. She went on chatting with Shelby over my head, discussing the big twist in a show I'd never seen, until Brianna and Hailey came back.

"Everyone ready?" Bri asked. "Chiara, almost done?"

"Done," she said, unplugging the curling iron. She shimmied off, carefree, like she hadn't just maimed me.

I reached for the burn, the skin there satiny, still hot.

"Onto the front porch!" Bri said, shepherding us outside. I noticed she was holding something behind her back.

"Ladies," she said. "I have some accessories. . . ."

In a dramatic reveal, she spun around and held up a set of silk sashes. Everyone clapped. Except for me, of course.

"Oh, God," I whispered to Jacqueline. "Are we going to have to wear those in public?"

"For the bride," Brianna said, presenting Hailey with a white sash that read, *Future Mrs. Poulter.*

"I love it!" Hailey said, pulling the sash over her head and smoothing it across her chest, beaming.

After her parents had divorced and her mom reverted to using her maiden name, Hailey told me that if she ever got married, she wouldn't take her husband's name. Thirteen years had passed since then and she was allowed to change her mind, but I wondered if the choice was conscious or a result of societal expectation. Maybe she worried if she kept her name, she'd have to field questions about why and then feel compelled to explain her deeply personal reasoning. She wouldn't have had to explain it to me. I understood. I bore witness to the unraveling of her family after her father left and to her mother's struggle to reclaim her independence, her own identity. So I couldn't help but feel a little uneasy watching Hailey proudly declare her status as the "Future Mrs. Poulter."

"For you," Brianna said, handing me a pink sash.

"Thanks."

I was about to put it on when I noticed that everyone's sash said something different. Brianna's read, *Maid of Dishonor*. Jacqueline's read, *Hot Mama*. Chiara's read, *Slay Queen*. Shelby's read, *Dancing Diva*.

I looked down, dread putting everything in slow motion. *Naughty Girl.*

Could have been worse, I thought. I swallowed my pride and slipped it on. I reluctantly posed for a group photo.

An Uber picked us up and took us to dinner. The restaurant was cool and casual, exposed brick and cozy booths under a tin ceiling. I appreciated the lack of pretense and happily ordered a cheeseburger.

Brianna insisted that we go around the table and tell our funniest Hailey story, which at first I thought was forced and corny, but it ended up being pretty entertaining. We laughed a lot. We drank pitchers of sangria.

When it came my turn to share a story, something surprising and unfortunate happened. I drew a blank. When everyone else was telling theirs, I sort of assumed that by the time it got to me, I would know what to say. I had so many stories to choose from. That time we went trick-or-treating a week before Halloween, stone-faced with confused neighbors. The time we commandeered my little cousin's Barbie Jeep and rode it through the Dunkin' Donuts drive-through. The time we faked breaking up in an Olive Garden. Somehow, on the spot, nothing seemed funny enough. It seemed impossible to convey how it had been in the moment. How hard we had laughed. So hard we couldn't breathe, we couldn't see. We laughed beyond sight, beyond sound. We were openmouthed and silent. We transcended.

"Come on, you know you have one," Chiara said.

Brianna added, "Don't be shy."

"I'm not shy. I'm thinking," I said, hooking my hand on the back of my neck, my fingers finding the burn. I wanted to tell them to come back to me, but I realized I was the last one to go. I looked over at Hailey, hoping for some assistance or an out. But she looked back at me expectantly. "This is too much pressure."

"It's no pressure," Brianna said. "Never mind. Don't worry."

"I'm not worried." As soon as I said it, as I heard myself say it, I knew I'd spoken too harshly. I followed up with a much softer "There's just so much history. We were kids together. We went to the same orthodontist."

"We did," Hailey said, picking an orange slice out of her sangria. "Tough times."

Jacqueline graciously changed the subject to Mike. "Let's roast the groom now, yeah?"

The rest of dinner went okay. I tried not to let the story thing bother me, but my efforts were futile because I was very bothered. Why award memories superlatives? Wasn't it enough to have them, to have lived them? Why play favorites? It was stupid.

Despite being steadfast in that belief, I felt guilty for not being able to harvest one to share. A shiny gem of a memory that beautifully reflected my friendship with Hailey and all the time we had spent together, all the fun we'd had. I felt not being able to do so invalidated that time somehow.

It also reminded me that those times were so far behind us, getting smaller and smaller in the rearview. What if they got so small that they disappeared altogether?

. . .

When we got back from the restaurant, I was too drunk and too tired to watch *Bridesmaids*. I knew if I verbalized my intention to go pass out in my clothes, I'd be met with peer pressure and/or disappointment. I could hear Hailey's voice in my head. *You're not going to watch the movie?*

So I slipped away without saying anything. I left them in the living room, Brianna taking a poll of who wanted popcorn. I went to the bathroom.

I balked at my reflection. My hair looked absurd. Big spiral curls, like I was a toddler pageant queen. I was mortified that I had spent the whole night like this, thinking I looked fine. How had I not noticed? Why had no one said anything? I wondered if it had been done to me maliciously. I wondered, *Are these fucking girls all out to get me? Is Hailey?*

I sighed, slipping the scrunchie from my wrist and pulling

back my hair, accidentally tying it up too tightly and straining the skin on my neck. My burn screamed. I loosened the scrunchie, but the pain lingered.

Curious to see the extent of my injury, I rooted through the makeup bag on the vanity. I found a compact and held it up, turning my back to the mirror over the sink and angling the compact to properly examine the back of my neck.

The burn was gnarlier than expected. A vicious smudge about the size, color, and texture of a peach pit. It was bad enough that I considered I might require burn gel. Aloe. Something. But I dreaded asking the group for help, knowing my need for medical attention would likely be viewed as a downer. I was already the "naughty girl," the bad seed, the odd one out.

I snapped the compact shut and returned it to the bag, then walked across the hall to my room, kicking off my shoes, rendering a single drunken hiccup before passing out facedown on my bed.

. . .

I woke up nine hours later to Brianna knocking on my door.

"Morning," she said. "We've got yoga in twenty!"

"All right," I grumbled. "I'll be there."

I put on leggings and a sports bra and went to the kitchen for water, drinking several glasses while watching birds flitter past the window.

The yoga instructor arrived a few minutes late. She was vivacious, tall, and muscular, and I think YouTube famous, but I didn't dare ask. I admired her septum piercing.

She brought mats and arranged them on the patio. We took our places and began our practice. The class was more intense than I'd anticipated.

"Sweat out all the toxins," the instructor said, looking right at me as if she could intuit that I was hungover.

I kept scanning my mat for bugs, kept feeling them on me. The creep of tiny legs, real or imagined.

Everyone else appeared to be seasoned yogis, masters of the crow pose, obscenely flexible. The exceptions were me, more into HIIT than vinyasa, and Hailey, whose elbow still gave her trouble after being broken in a car accident eight years ago. My mat was positioned behind hers, and at one point I could tell she was really struggling with a pose, so I leaned forward and whispered, "Please don't fart."

She burst out laughing.

Our goofing continued to escalate from there, much to Brianna's irritation.

After class, we took turns showering and reconvened in

the kitchen. Bri was there, still in her yoga clothes, frying some eggs.

"Do you need help?" I asked her.

She already had Shelby washing berries and Chiara scooping batter into a waffle iron, so I expected her to say no, but she said, "Yes, actually. Can you get out the juice? And can you set the table? Plates and glasses and silverware. Just make sure they're all clean."

"Sure," I said.

"And maybe more coffee."

I wondered if assigning me multiple chores was punishment for my yoga mischief. I did as I was asked, and was feeling confident that I'd redeemed myself until, as I was carrying a carafe of OJ to the table, someone screamed. A sudden, bloodcurdling, nails-on-the-chalkboard, horror-movie scream. Startled, I jerked my arms back, spilling juice all over my shirt.

I spun around and locked eyes with Shelby, who was standing coolly at the counter, decapitating a strawberry. She gave a single-shoulder shrug and said, "Thought I saw a spider."

"Oh. Okay . . ."

She shrugged again, then changed the subject. "These strawberries are so perfect. So *ripe*."

Bri was concentrating on the eggs, and Chiara was searching for something in the fridge. Neither of them had flinched at Shelby's scream. There seemed to be zero concern, zero acknowledgment.

Because they're fucking with you, I thought.

"Did you spill?" Bri asked, finally looking up from the stove.

"A little. It's fine," I said.

I sat through brunch sticky and smelling like citrus.

"Thank you so much for making all of this," Hailey said.

"Of course, of course," Brianna said. "It's your weekend."

"It's perfect. Thanks, Bri. Thanks, everyone."

"It's just getting started! I've still got some more tricks up my sleeve. Some fun little surprises, and one big, *epic* surprise," she said with a wink.

I predicted a stripper. Then I remembered the box I had seen in Bri's trunk, and the rope, and wondered if it was something really kinky, some *Fifty Shades of Grey* cosplay shit, but I figured they were probably all too vanilla.

"You're the best," Hailey said, blowing Brianna a kiss. Brianna blew one back. They carried on volleying ethereal kisses.

As I watched them, I battled an abrupt wave of nausea. The squirmy feeling was back. An overwhelming unease.

I want to go home, I thought. *I want to leave right now. I should just leave.*

Everyone else at the table was happily salting their eggs and passing the syrup. The isolation of my distress only made it seem more urgent.

Relax, I told myself. *Another twenty-four hours and you'll be on the train home. You can tough it out. It's fine. Everything's fine.*

I got up to make myself another mimosa.

"Anyone else want one?" I asked.

They all did.

• • •

Because of the brunch mimosas, I became the default bartender for the rest of the day. I kept getting requests, so I kept making drinks. It gave me something to do. It gave me purpose.

It also made me popular.

"You make such good drinks," Chiara said after I mixed her a mojito.

"This is soooo good, Natalie!" Shelby said after a sip of her negroni.

I made Jacqueline a few martinis. I made Hailey a Moscow mule. I made Brianna mad.

"We have to pace ourselves!" she kept saying as we kept drinking. "Nat, don't make them too strong."

We spent most of the afternoon on the porch, talking and swatting at mosquitoes. Some of the conversations were too steeped in college nostalgia for me or Jacqueline to participate in, which might have been irksome, had I not been pleasantly tipsy. Also, I understood the need for "remember when."

My relationship with Hailey was ninety-five percent "remember when." That's how it is with old friends. You rely on the past for sustenance. If months pass where you don't speak, or if a year goes by without seeing each other, it's okay because you still have that precious supply of shared experiences.

I tried not to think about whether it was a sustainable model. If one day, our memories alone wouldn't be enough to hold us anymore. Hailey and I had always been different. I was rambunctious and opinionated. I started arguments with teachers, broke the dress code, got detention. Hailey was more agreeable, sunny, and beloved, a star athlete, captain of the soccer team. I was uncoordinated but an exceptional student, 4.0 GPA. She struggled in class. I was desperate to get out of our hometown; she still attended our high school's football games after graduating. She was a romantic obsessed with Jane Austen; I turned off *Pride and Prejudice* after realizing we never get to see them bang. I tried to get her to read Orwell, talk politics, but she was uninterested. She craved peace and structure and had a specific vision for her life, aspired to the traditional trajectory of marriage, house, kids. I craved freedom, wanted to live in a big city, to be surrounded by art and culture and noise and garbage and possibility. Our dreams were each other's nightmares. But it was fine. We weren't friends because we had a lot in common, or because our goals or interests were aligned. We were friends of adolescent circumstance, friends because we had fun together. We were friends because we loved each other.

I took a sip of my whiskey ginger and studied her. We were fast approaching twilight, and she squinted into the plummeting sun, smiling and laughing and continuously adjusting her engagement ring, a big gaudy thing she posted too many pictures of with captions like so obsessed and so lucky. I suspected it wasn't a fair-trade diamond.

We were friends because we had met when we were young, and when you're young, it doesn't really matter how different you are. The world isn't complicated yet, and neither are you.

• • •

At around six o'clock, a white van pulled up and out popped a petite woman dressed in all black. She had an assistant with her, a girl with large glasses and pastel hair.

Brianna went down to greet them.

"I'm going to go change," I said, an excuse to get out of the way of whatever was about to be happening.

"I'll walk inside with you," Hailey said. "I have to pee."

She threaded her arm through mine, and we skipped into the house together.

"Are you having fun?" she asked me.

"Yeah," I lied. "Of course."

"Good," she said, her voice a little squeaky.

I knew I shouldn't, but I asked anyway. "Why?"

"Oh, well, you skipped the movie last night."

"Sorry. I was zonked. I didn't know it was a requirement."

"It wasn't. I was just worried. . . ."

"You don't need to worry about me," I said. "I'm here. I'm game. I'm a barrel of laughs."

"As long as you're having a good time. It's important to me. I know it's *my* weekend, but I want everyone to enjoy it."

I couldn't tell if she was being serious or facetious, referring to it as "*my* weekend." It troubled me that I couldn't make the distinction, that I wasn't able to read her anymore.

"Okay, I really need to pee," she said. "Love you."

"Love you, too."

"Try to let loose, Nat. Participate!" she said as she disappeared into the powder room.

The interaction irritated me. I thought I had been participating. I wasn't sure what else she wanted from me. What more could I possibly do?

A bitterness took root.

I decided to take another shower to really draw out my getting-ready process. I was used to washing myself with a loofah, but since I didn't have one, I had to use my hands. As I moved the lather over my body, I felt the awkward knobs of my knees, the prickly spot on my calf that I always missed when shaving. I felt the scar on the inside of my thigh, which I had gotten New Year's Eve senior year of high school when Hailey and I split a bottle of Malibu and ran around her neighborhood at midnight in our pajamas. For reasons unknown, I mounted one of those decorative deer made of Christmas lights. I hadn't expected it to be so sharp, but I was too drunk to care about the injury. I still can't believe it left a scar.

I thought maybe I should have told that story at dinner the night before, but it was one of those things where you really had to be there.

Only Hailey would have understood.

. . .

After showering, blowing out my hair, reapplying my makeup, changing into my hot pink bachelorette dress, and a solid twenty minutes on my phone reading articles about products celebrities couldn't live without, I took a deep breath and opened the door.

It was like I had emerged into a completely different house. There were flowers everywhere, candles everywhere. The lights were dimmed. I heard voices, but I couldn't tell where they were coming from. The air smelled of rosemary.

There was no one in the kitchen, no one in the living room. There was no one on the front porch. The white van was still parked on the driveway, but there was no one inside.

I went back into the house and slipped on my shoes. I peered out of a back window and saw a vague glow, ribbons of light coming from somewhere. Maybe the patio.

I grabbed my cardigan out of my suitcase and went out the back door.

There was a canopy of string lights over an extravagantly set dining table. Gorgeous floral centerpieces, jewel-toned glassware, artfully mismatched plates. There was music all around, gently emanating from hidden speakers.

"Well, isn't this magical?" I asked.

No one looked up to acknowledge my presence. They continued talking amongst themselves. They were huddled in close, drinking pale pink liquid out of mason jars. There was fruit drowning inside.

"Hey," I said, trying to get Hailey's attention. She was laughing maniacally at something, leaning on Brianna's shoulder.

No one else had dressed up. I felt foolish.

"Hey," Jacqueline said, giving me a slight nod and then returning to her conversation with Chiara.

There was a sudden divorce of nerves. Part of me was salty, indignant. They had been keen to include me that afternoon when I was making them drinks. Now that I was no longer of service, they were being rude to me. That was rich.

But the other part of me was panicked and sad. I was completely alone. I was staring at someone I considered a sister, and she was too preoccupied to notice me. I wondered if she even cared that I was there. I wondered if I hadn't shown up, if she would have missed me.

The anger and the insecurity manifested in a strange, pathetic decision.

I cleared my throat as loudly as I could. Then I said, "A shame Dana couldn't be here."

That got everyone's attention. Especially Bri's.

I regretted it immediately. I wasn't sure what possessed me to be so openly vindictive. I wanted to blame Brianna for instigating it, but I knew in that moment it wasn't her fault. It was mine.

I also knew that I could not, would not, show any sign of my escalating vulnerability. The crowd was silent in their shock, and Brianna stumbled backward slightly. I could see beyond her a small round table that had more of the mason jar drinks on it. I went over and helped myself to one.

"Look at you," Chiara said, her tone indecipherable.

"Cute dress," Shelby said.

"Glad you decided to join us!" Brianna said, smiling. "Just in time. First course should be served momentarily."

Right then the girl with the pastel hair reappeared, carrying a massive bowl of salad.

"Let's sit!" Brianna said. "There are place cards, so find your name."

It was fairly obvious to me that Brianna was behind the seating arrangements. Hailey was at the head of the table, Brianna at her left, Chiara at her right. Shelby was next to Chiara, Jacqueline next to Brianna. Then me, the other head. I was facing Hailey, but we were too far away to converse, and there was a giant flower arrangement in the way.

We sat down and began to pass around the salad bowl.

I anticipated another toast, but there wasn't one. Or maybe there had been, but I'd missed it.

Shelby began interviewing Jacqueline about parenthood, and the two of them conversed across me throughout both the salad course and the main course of vegetable Wellington.

I was excavating an unwanted mushroom when Jacqueline turned to me and said, "You're quiet."

It's absolutely insufferable when someone tells you you're being quiet when actually you're being ignored.

"Just listening," I said.

"Do you want kids?" Shelby asked me.

I shrugged. "Haven't thought about it."

"You're single," Jacqueline said. It wasn't a question, but I answered it like one.

"Yeah," I said. "I'm single."

"Enjoy the freedom," Jacqueline said, sipping her wine. I'd already finished my wine and given up hope for a refill. "You'll find someone when you least expect it."

"God, I don't miss being single," Shelby said, forking a tomato. She dropped her utensil and gasped. "Oh, I'm so sorry. I didn't mean ..."

"You're fine," I said.

I wanted to defend my life, talk about how much I loved

it exactly as it was. I loved my apartment, my job, my neighborhood. I loved going out on a Saturday night and chatting up strangers, meeting new people, staying out until four in the morning. I loved doing whatever I wanted and not having to answer to anyone.

I wanted to tell her it was okay if she pitied me for not having a husband, because I pitied her for having one. I wanted to say, *You committed to sleeping with one person for the rest of your life. How does that honestly make you feel?*

But I figured it was best to just stay quiet.

"I think you're the only true bachelorette here," Jacqueline said.

"Groovy," I said. "Is there going to be dessert?"

There was. A three-tiered chocolate-and-raspberry cake. Brianna cut slices for everyone. I thought mine was a little small.

I was chewing my last raspberry when Brianna began clinking her glass with her knife.

"Ladies, ladies," she said. "I hope you enjoyed this wonderful dinner, but the night is young! If you will please now follow me inside, I have something very special planned. . . ."

Hailey began to giggle. "What is it?"

Chiara shook her head. "I genuinely don't know."

"Me either," Shelby said. "Seriously."

"That's because it's a *surprise*," Brianna said. She stood up and set her napkin down over her plate. "Come, come!"

She turned and took Hailey's hand, who took Chiara's, who took Shelby's, who reached for mine and I gave it to her. I reached for Jacqueline, but she had already started walking toward the house.

Brianna led us inside, to a door in the main hallway that I had assumed was a closet.

"Okay," she said, giddy and unhinged. Her cheeks had inflated; her eyes bulged. Her smile spread to her ears. It looked as though her features were in danger of bursting off her face.

I was certain she was about to open the door to reveal a beefy dude in a fireman's uniform. But instead, she opened the door to nothing. To inky darkness.

I realized then that at some point she'd acquired a candle. She was holding a lit taper candle, set on a small plate with a round handle, like something out of a period drama.

I couldn't help it. I started to laugh.

"Where did you get that?" I asked.

She shot me a look of pure venom.

"Nat," Hailey said. There was a starkness to her voice that I found upsetting. It made me feel like a child.

She'd never used that tone with me before.

"Follow me," Brianna said with an exaggerated wink.

Everyone else followed, so I did, too. We followed her down a staircase. It seemed unsafe to descend stairs in almost total darkness, but I had exhausted my spunk and knew there was no point in bringing it up. I held a hand to the wall to help steady myself. It was stony and cold.

When I got to the bottom, I shuffled toward the pale glow of Brianna's candle.

As my eyes adjusted, phantom shapes traversed my vision. There was a draft. I heard a dripping somewhere. It smelled of mildew. The ceiling was so low I had to hunch over slightly.

Brianna struck a match. She began moving around, lighting candles. The more candles she lit, the more the scene came into view. A dank, unfinished basement. Empty except for the candles, except for . . .

My dinner threatened resurrection.

There was a small round table draped in black velvet. On it was the wooden box I'd seen the day before in Bri's trunk, along with the rope and a large golden chalice. The table was perfectly centered in a symbol that appeared to have been spray-painted on the floor. I would have described the symbol as pentagram adjacent.

I found what was before me deeply disturbing but held out hope it was an elaborate prank.

"Oh, my God! Yes!" Chiara said. "Yes!"

"You didn't!" Shelby shrieked. "I always wanted to do this! So bummed I missed out at my bachelorette."

"Brianna," Hailey said. "Brianna."

"I know, I know," Bri said. "It's extra."

I tried to discern Hailey's expression. It was too difficult in the faint, fuzzy candlelight.

"No," Hailey said. "I mean, it is. But I love it. So freaking cool!"

"This is awesome," Jacqueline said. "Well done, Bri."

"Sorry," I said. "Are we about to summon demons or something?"

Everyone laughed. I experienced a brief flash of relief, thinking the "gotcha" was soon to follow.

"Oh, gosh. No," Bri said. "Close but no."

"Excuse me," I said. "Close? What do you mean, *close*?"

"It's an offering ritual," Hailey said, "using a summoning cup. You've never heard of it?"

"Um, no."

"Oh," Chiara said. "They're really common now. New bachelorette tradition."

"Well, old tradition, technically," Jacqueline said. "It's an ancient bridal ritual."

"You've seriously never heard of this?" Hailey asked.

"You're messing with me, right?" I held my head in my

hands to make sure it was screwed on straight. My thumb moved to the burn at the base of my skull. The skin peeled. "No, I've never heard of a cup ritual."

"I guess you haven't been to any bachelorette parties recently," Hailey said. "But it's a thing. Trust me. They're all over Pinterest. The kits are just superhard to get, so this is, like, so crazy. I can't believe you got one, Bri! I love you!"

She threw her arms around Brianna and squeezed.

"Anything for you, babe. So, how it works, for those who don't know."

She looked directly at me.

"Hailey will go around counterclockwise and ask each of us for an offering, a gift. Something unique to us that she can take with her into her marriage. Usually, it's a trait-slash-quality that she admires about that person. Like, for me, Hailey might ask me to offer my gift of planning fun events. I will agree to the offering, giving verbal confirmation. Then Hailey will cut my palm, using the sacred blade, and I'll squeeze just a few drops of blood into the summoning cup. After we've all pledged our gifts and made our blood sacrifice, we'll join hands around Hailey as she drinks from the cup and ingests our gifts, summoning them into her life and into her spirit. And yeah! Then we'll go upstairs and continue the party!"

I couldn't speak. My mouth was so dry it was like I'd

swallowed sand. I looked at Jacqueline, whom I considered the most rational of the bunch, but she seemed absolutely unfazed.

"Everyone good?" Brianna asked. "Let me get the music on and we can get started."

"Wait," I said.

They all turned to me, eager, just like they had at dinner the night before when I struggled to produce a funny anecdote. I felt this grave pressure to articulate, but I couldn't form the words. They were serious. This was serious. It was so ludicrous; I didn't know where to start. I wanted to tell them they were all out of their fucking minds, but they were acting so supremely chill about everything that I couldn't help but question myself. Was I overreacting?

"It's gonna be cool, Nat. I promise," Hailey said. "I've heard it's a great bonding experience."

Were we not already bonded?

"You really want to do this?" I asked her.

"Yes," she said, smiling. "Definitely."

"You want to drink blood?"

She shrugged. "It's no big deal. People eat placenta."

"I did," Jacqueline said. "I ate mine. It's good for you."

"Uh, not quite the same thing," I argued.

"Are we ready?" Bri asked, clearly growing impatient.

She didn't wait for a response. She disappeared into some shadowy corner of the basement, and I saw her phone illuminate. It was plugged into a portable speaker that was surprisingly powerful, considering its size. The song that began to play was loud and intense. It sounded suspiciously similar to the *Game of Thrones* theme.

"Let us gather," Brianna said. She opened the wooden box and pulled out a legit dagger. It had an intricate handle, and the blade was etched with symbols like the one painted on the floor. "Is anyone here squeamish?"

"What's the rope for?" I asked, because it was there on the table and obviously had a purpose, and I couldn't stand not knowing what it was.

"The rope is for Hailey. She'll bind our hands before she cuts us. Prevents wriggling. Wouldn't want any accidents. Plus, it's just, like, part of the ritual. Okay, Nat?"

"Um . . ."

I could feel them staring at me, their eyes like piranhas. It seemed so archaic. I could barely accept the concept of a bridal shower, gifting expensive stand mixers and custom cutting boards and fucking Dutch ovens and robot vacuums for assistance with wifely duties. How was I supposed to get behind this? And how was I the only one horrified by it?

Participate, Hailey had said to me earlier. *Participate*.

"Fine, I guess," I said. "Let's just do it."

Brianna's eyebrows elevated. I realized she had expected for me to opt out, and this made me want to do it more.

"Okeydoke," she said. She took a deep breath. "We are here tonight to honor our most cherished friend, Hailey Bankman, who will soon be entering the sanctity of marriage. We wish to offer her our best, most precious gifts, and are willing to sacrifice so that the universe may bear witness to our loyalty and devotion. . . ."

Had I not been so determined, I might have laughed at Brianna's whole little speech. I was too busy convincing myself that it wasn't that big of a deal. It was like a cholesterol finger-prick test. A few drops of blood, and I could move on with my life.

Hailey went up to Brianna first. She bound Bri's hands with the rope, giggling a little as she attempted to tie the knot. Brianna remained serious.

"I ask you, Brianna Engle, for an offering of creativity," Hailey said. "Will you give me this gift?"

"I will," Brianna said.

Without hesitation, Hailey lifted the dagger and brought it down swiftly across Bri's palm. I was stunned at the vibrance of the blood, at the aggressiveness of its blossom. It dripped into the chalice with a sickening splash.

Brianna nodded solemnly, and then Hailey moved on to Shelby, who I realized was standing beside me. I wasn't sure how that happened, how I'd come to be next. I wished I'd been more strategic in my placement in the circle. I wished I had more time.

"I ask you, Shelby Martino, for an offering of optimism. Will you give me this gift?"

"I will, of course!"

I knew something went wrong right away, even though I'd been distracted scrutinizing the painted symbol. It was the sound Shelby made. A sharp gasp followed by a whimpering breath.

There was too much blood. It gushed. Hailey had cut too deep. She knew it. Everyone knew it. The vibe shifted.

I thought, *This is it. It's gone too far. They're gonna call it.*

But no one said anything.

I felt completely detached from reality. I felt like I was in a dream. I closed my eyes, and with only the music, I felt like I was about to find out what betrayals were going down in Westeros.

It's for Hailey, I said to myself. *For the sake of our friendship. Just do it for Hailey.*

Do it for the girl who took you to McDonald's after you lost your virginity and bought you a McFlurry, and when you started to cry because you felt different, she told you everything was going to be all right. That it was only a hymen.

Do it for the girl who crimped your hair for junior prom, where you ended up ditching your dates to slow dance together to "The Reason" by Hoobastank. You sang along obnoxiously. You clutched each other's faces as you held out the notes.

Do it for the girl who put sunscreen on your back all those hot summer Saturdays at the Hackettstown pool, who didn't judge you for that one time you threw up after eating too much Domino's, just laughed and said, "It happens."

I wanted to. I wanted to do it for that girl. But I knew. That girl and the girl I used to be were both gone. We were women now, fully realized, with our own wants and needs and values. We were women, and we were ghosts. I was a ghost in Hailey's life, and she was a ghost in mine. We'd been pretending, running on fumes for years, holding on to a fading friendship for the sake of our past selves. I could no longer continue in denial; I could no longer ignore the unsavory truth.

Because there I was in a room full of strangers, about to compromise myself, scar myself physically and emotionally for someone I didn't know anymore. Someone who was gleefully tying my wrists with rope.

It wasn't fair for her to ask this of me. She saw that I

was uncomfortable, and she had pressured me into it as a "bonding experience." Even if she did honestly believe that and it wasn't a manipulation tactic to get me to play along, that didn't make it okay. None of it was okay.

The dagger gleamed in candlelight.

Not o-fucking-kay.

"I ask you, Natalie Lewis, for an offering of—"

"No," I said, slipping my hands from the binding. Luckily, the knot was loose. "I don't want to do this. I can't."

"Nat," Hailey said.

"Seriously?" Brianna asked. "The ritual already started!"

"Hailey, I'm sorry, but this is ridiculous. Can't you see that? Can't you snap out of it for one second and realize this is a bit much?"

"This isn't about *you* and what *you* think," Bri snapped. "This is about Hailey. God! At least Dana had the decency to sit it out instead of ruining the entire ritual."

"Is this why Dana didn't come?" I asked. "I thought her mom broke her jaw."

"Well, I mean, yeah. That was the, like, main factor," Bri stuttered. She was holding her hand over her head to stop the bleeding. "But she also has, like, a blood disorder. So she couldn't participate anyway. I asked. I checked."

"Aw, Dana," Hailey said.

"She would have done it," Brianna said, "if not for health reasons."

"You're all certifiable," I said. "I'm not going to let you gaslight me into thinking this is normal, because it's not! This is some dark, cult-y, vampire bullshit. Also, it doesn't seem sanitary."

"Please, Nat," Hailey pleaded, her eyes wide. "This means *so* much to me."

I resisted the urge to turn away and instead let my gaze linger on Hailey, waiting for the tug of guilt, for a heaviness in my chest. Remorse. But I didn't feel anything. In the erratic flickers of candlelight, I could barely recognize her.

There was no guilt. No sadness. Nothing, not anymore. Why mourn what was already lost?

I opened my mouth to speak but was interrupted by a weary groan. Shelby. She was covered in blood. *Covered.* Hailey had really botched the cut.

"She probably needs stitches," I said. "I already *ruined* the ritual, so why don't we take Shelby to urgent care? Unless you want to ask the universe if it can take care of this."

"I'm fine," Shelby slurred, her eyes rolling back. She took a teetering step forward, then fell. The sound her head made when it found the floor echoes in my nightmares.

Jacqueline rushed toward her, turning her over onto her back. She flopped like a dead fish. She was out cold.

"Is she okay?" Hailey asked.

"Yeah, she's great," I said, surrendering to sarcasm.

"I cannot *believe* this!" Bri. Of course.

"Should I call nine-one-one?" Chiara asked. "Should we try to get her to the car?"

"I'll call nine-one-one," Jacqueline said. "Can someone get her some gauze? A cold compress? Does anyone have a first aid kit? Is there one in the house?"

"I'll check," I said, already halfway up the stairs. I pretended I didn't hear Bri when she called after me, saying she knew where the kit was and would get it herself.

I don't know when exactly I made the decision to leave, or if I even made it at all. I'd like to think I would have actually searched for the kit had Brianna not taken over, but it's hard to say. Next thing I knew, I was packing my things hurriedly and requesting an Uber to take me to the station, where the last train to Grand Central was leaving in half an hour.

Thankfully, the driver was there waiting for me when I snuck out the front door. He was a chatty man in a fedora. My knight in shining armor.

"How's your Saturday?" he asked me.

"Weird," I answered.

"Oh." He laughed. "How about that?"

He then proceeded to tell me about his bunions for the rest of the ride.

I was relieved by the solitude of the station. I stood on the platform staring at the sky, shifting my weight from foot to foot, exhaling my adrenaline.

I turned my phone off. I figured they would gather that I bailed, and I wasn't ready to face the fallout. I'd suffered enough.

When the train came, I stumbled on and found an open seat near a window. I pressed my forehead against the cool glass and tried not to think about anything that had happened.

I tried not to think about the ritual, how fucked up it was.

I tried not to think about stupid Bri. I tried not to think about Shelby, about all the blood.

I tried not to think about Hailey and the friendship that I had let expire in that basement.

I tried not to think about how sad I would have been if I'd known at fourteen, when she and I would stay up late stargazing in her yard, that one day we would drift so far, we'd split apart.

I tried not to think about how she would look on her wedding day, in that ivory mermaid gown that I told her

I liked because everyone else at the appointment liked it, though really, I thought it didn't suit her as well as the lace A-line. I tried not to picture her walking down the aisle with her bouquet of yellow daffodils, walking toward a life without me in it.

I stared down at my hands, my open palms unscathed, and hoped that someday I could forgive her for what she was willing to sacrifice and that she could forgive me for what I wasn't.

GOBLIN

IT WAS DANI'S IDEA to download the Goblin. We were in the dressing room at H&M and she kept sending me out for different sizes. I passed her multiple pairs of the same jeans through the curtain as the attendant disapproved from behind a rack of unwanted clothes.

"None of my clothes fit," Dani said as she pulled me into her room. "I found this incredible dress to wear to Michelle and Ben's wedding, but I don't feel good in it. You know what I mean?"

"Mm," I said, stumbling over a pile of skinny high-rises.

"I need to lose five pounds," she said. "Will you do it with me? I do better with a partner. I heard it's super easy. You just download the app and you get a Goblin."

"Is it tech or magic?"

She shrugged.

Some people are good at saying no. Toddlers are good at saying no. Virgins are good at saying no. God is good at saying no. I am not good at saying no.

She said we'd start on Monday. *Poor Monday,* I thought. *It's the Ringo of days.*

I reconsidered my decision later that night, letting the shower run hot so the bathroom filled with steam and diluted the light, making it kinder to my body. I used to shower in the dark, but then I got into the habit of feeling myself with my hands and misimagining my proportions. *Are my thighs really that wide? My hips?* Eventually, I relented and turned the lights back on. I couldn't go on cutting myself shaving. My shins looked like butcher block.

I counted the little pink scars as I sat on the edge of the tub, wrapped in a towel, my toes swirling the soap suds roving toward the drain. I thought about calling Dani and politely backing out of the diet. The only problem was, I wouldn't know how to answer if she asked me why.

Well. Not the only problem. My plucky past self had committed to going to this wedding. Stuffed the RSVP in the mail with the stunning arrogance of a white-collar criminal. Four months ago, I had been certain this wedding was the perfect opportunity to prove to myself that I was finally over him. To be in the same room and for once not feel like an unwanted puppy, like a sad footnote in someone else's love story.

A few weeks out, I wasn't feeling so confident. But it was too late now. I'd committed. Chosen salmon over chicken. What would they think if I didn't show?

. . .

On Sunday night I spent two hours debating whether or not I should order Chinese food before ordering Chinese food. The weeks ahead of me loomed in the image of a giant undressed salad. Of course I caved. Sesame chicken with brown and white rice, pork lo mein, wonton soup, an egg roll. They threw in those flavorless crunchy noodles, and I ate them mindlessly, dunking them in duck sauce. There were two fortune cookies, which meant they assumed there would be two people eating the food.

My first fortune said, *Joys are often the shadows cast by sorrows.* I was too traumatized to open the second.

I ate until it was painful, until I had to lie on my side to stop from feeling like I was going to burst. I messaged Dani. Last supper?

Bottle of Rosé. To. My. Face.

Naughty.

You?

I eyed the catastrophe strewn about my coffee table. The empty container of chicken, the stray noodles drooping over the side of the grease-stained take-out box, used napkins and leaky sauce packets oozing soy onto the ripped paper bag it all came in. A few crumbs of crunchy noodles powdered the wreckage.

I replied, Noodles.

Nice.

I threw everything away. Took out the garbage. Cleaned the coffee table with a Lysol wipe, lit a candle to mask the smell.

I'll make it up tomorrow, I told myself, washing my hands like Lady Macbeth. *Gym and juice cleanse. Tomorrow.*

• • •

Dani came over after work to download the app. We planned to start the diet first thing but decided to wait to get the app until we were together. We were too afraid to do it alone. I had only seen what the Goblin looked like in ads. Cute and animated. Smurf-esque. "Gotta get a Goblin!"

I resisted Googling to avoid the opinions of hangry strangers. Dieters aren't reliable, always quick to jump on bandwagons only to abandon them twice as fast. Atkins. South Beach. Master cleanse. Gluten free. Paleo. Whole30. Until the studies find you should really base your diet on your blood type. Until other studies find that's bullshit.

Dani showed up in head-to-toe Adidas, a smoothie in each hand. All I'd eaten that day was oatmeal and cucumber slices. I was grateful for the smoothie but also wanted to smack it out of her hand.

We sat at my kitchen table, holding our phones. We opened the app store. It was the second-most-popular Goblin app, coming in after Goblin Quest.

"Ready?"

"It's four ninety-nine?"

"Meg."

"Okay, okay."

We pressed our thumbs and waited.

Two tiny green Goblins appeared, each about six inches tall. Dani's was wearing a nightcap and glittery shoes with little bells. It twirled, shook its hips side to side, and gave her the thumbs-up. Dani giggled with delight. "Cute!" she said.

I felt my face fall. My Goblin was stocky. He wore an unbuttoned vest and clunky brown boots. His head was shiny and bald except for three thick, curly black hairs spiraling up like springs. His ears were the size of quarters, paler than the rest of him and pointy. The worst part about him was his mouth. He had fangs, two sharp canines poking out of his flat gray lips. His arms were crossed over his chest.

"Mine looks angry," I said.

"Aw, no! He's just serious. Means business." Dani rested her chin on the table. "Hello, little ones."

"What now?" I asked, but before the words were out, the Goblins were gone.

"They'll come back when we need them."

"Like when?"

"Like when we're about to make a bad choice," she said. "Like order Chinese."

She lifted my fortune off the counter. I thought I'd thrown it out.

"Last supper," I said. "Noodles. I told you."

"I know," she said, her voice like helium. "I wasn't shaming."

I picked at a chip in my manicure, pretended I wasn't bothered.

"Want to watch a movie or something?" she asked.

In the movie we watched, the actress was very thin.

. . .

I woke up to panic. There was commotion in my apartment. Crash. Bang. Slam. *I might die right where I am,* I thought, standing in my bedroom in mismatched flannel pajamas and slippers shaped like narwhals. I always think I'd be good in a crisis until I'm in a crisis; then I remember the truth about myself.

Something glowed in my periphery. There was a message illuminating the belly of my phone. The message said, Hi, Gorgeous! Your Goblin is visiting, doing some Goblin good!

I stepped cautiously out of my bedroom. The light was on in the kitchen. I paused in the doorway, a force field of equal parts shock and fear stopping me from going in.

There it was, ripping through my cabinets. It poured out a box of reduced-fat Cheez-Its and started stomping, crushing them into orange dust.

"Hey!" I yelled from the doorway.

It looked up at me, its small, dark eyes narrowing. Then it went back to its destruction. It hopped over to the fridge, pulled the door open, and climbed inside. Before I fully understood what I was doing, I slammed the refrigerator door shut.

From inside I heard a horrible, guttural grunting, then a distinct *pop!*

The Goblin was on the floor by my right foot. It glowered at my slipper for a moment, then drew its arm back and slapped my slipper across its adorable narwhal face. The Goblin wiped its hands on its vest, walked over to the fridge, opened it, and continued its work. Stunned, I sat myself down at the table with a glass of water.

I watched as it marched across the floor with a chocolate bar lifted over its head. The Goblin tossed it into the garbage, along with a bag of frozen chicken fingers, a half-empty jar of Alfredo sauce, ranch dip, and a carton of chocolate soy milk.

The Goblin vanished after it finished clearing out the fridge. I shuffled back to bed but couldn't calm myself enough to sleep. I tried all my usual tricks. Breathing exercises. Naming state capitals and all of the kids in my kindergarten class. Selecting a memory and re-creating the scene in my mind in great detail. My fifth-birthday party with a clown called Annie who wore an orange wig and a felt dress and who made popcorn in her hat.

It was no use. My mind insisted on going back to the one thing, the one person, I was trying not to think about.

I wondered if he looked the same as he did back in college, his hair long, fuzz on his face, a little over his lip and a little under. I wondered if he was as skinny as he used to be, if he wore the same clothes: baggy T-shirts he bought already ripped, black jeans, scuffed-up combat boots with the laces loose. I remember the distinct thud his boots made when they hit my dorm room floor. Conjuring the sound still got me excited.

His mouth was always cold for some reason, and when he kissed me, I would get the chills. He thought he was turning me on, and he was, but mostly I was cold. I'd pull him onto me for body heat.

One time he told me he loved me. He didn't mean to. I woke up in his room on a brutal February morning after promising myself I'd never go there again, but there I was, staring at the tapestry he had tacked to his ceiling. Stars twirling around the signs of the zodiac. He's a Capricorn. I should have known. My high school boyfriend was a Capricorn. He took my virginity and treated me like garbage. Told me I should get a tan. The worst part about it was I did. I went tanning. If I get skin cancer someday, I'll scream.

"Hey, be back soon. Love you."

Right away, he realized what he'd done. I saw it on his face.

"Okay," I said, pulling the covers over my shoulder, pretending I was still mostly asleep. I stayed in his bed a while longer, trying to remember everything I'd learned in psychology class about Freudian slips.

He's the only one I ever told about my treatment. I figured he'd understand because he has two sisters, and because I knew it wouldn't make a difference if I told him or not. He wouldn't want me either way.

"It's something I still struggle with," I said.

"I'm sorry," he said, holding my head to his chest, kissing my forehead. He smelled like tobacco and Axe. "You're beautiful."

I thought, *That's it?*

. . .

For me, the hunger was nostalgia. It was like visiting an old friend, a friend I'd forgotten how much I hated.

But I had overcome hunger before. I knew I was capable. I knew I could starve.

It spawned in my gut around eight thirty every morning that first week. By noon my vision spotted and shoulders wilted. My lunch was three plain rice cakes, grapes, and nonfat peach yogurt. By the time I left work, I wanted to strangle everything that moved. I stampeded through my apartment door and heated some sodium-light tomato soup on the stove top, ate it with spelt toast. Every night, *every night*, I burned my tongue on that godforsaken soup. I couldn't wait for it to cool.

I had apple slices with cinnamon for dessert.

I was highly motivated. I wanted to look good for Ben. There was the backless dress I'd ordered for the wedding, the picture of Emily Ratajkowski I'd taped to my fridge.

Really, I just didn't want the Goblin to come back.

I weighed myself at the gym, breaking a dusty old promise I'd made to myself, my parents, various therapists. The numbers were mean.

My stomach bloated in protest. I pressed my fingers down on it and made my skin pale. I went to bed early.

On Sunday I went to McDonald's. Fast and dirty. I stood in line salivating at the smell of salt and crackling hot oil. I had to wipe the corners of my mouth with my sleeve. I ordered a ten-piece chicken nugget and ate them out of my jacket pockets on the walk home. I was on my third when the Goblin appeared. He slapped the nugget out of my hand.

"Hey!" I said.

"Hey!" he said. His voice was gruff and ugly.

He reached into my jacket and began throwing the nuggets onto the ground one by one. I managed to save two and shove them into my mouth. He glared at me with his beady black eyes, climbed up my arm, stood on my shoulder, and tried to pry open my mouth. He dug his fingernails into my lip.

"Ow!" The chicken mush came spilling out, landing mostly on my chin.

I shook the Goblin off. I expected him to go flying but he landed on the sidewalk before me on both feet, his hands on his hips.

I wiped away the half-chewed nuggets with the back of my hand.

"Jerk."

"Bitch."

He began to kick the dirty ground nuggets into a nearby sewer grate, muttering to himself. When the last nugget was gone, he disappeared.

I called Dani.

She was out of breath. "I'm on the elliptical. What's up?"

"My Goblin called me a bitch!"

She laughed.

"I'm serious!"

"They can't talk."

"I swear to God it just called me a bitch."

"Mine doesn't say anything."

"Lucky you."

"Maybe you get the Goblin that suits you," she panted. "You respond better to tough love."

"No, I don't."

"You always date mean men."

"Who was mean?"

"Kurt. Milo. Ben. Your high school boyfriend."

"Ben wasn't mean," I said. "I was in love with him and he was in love with someone else. That's different."

"Sure. I have to go. I'll call you later."

We hung up and I moped home. I found my workout clothes laid out for me on my bed, my sneakers on my pillows. There was a package torn open on the floor, and the dress I'd bought for the wedding was hanging on the door to my closet, slinky and beautiful and small. It fluttered in the breeze from the open window. It looked like it was dancing.

I wanted to be angry, but I could feel the grease lingering on my chin and was disgusted with myself. I'd begun to undress when I saw the Goblin out of the corner of my eye, a smear of green disappearing. I turned to see where it went, but instead I saw myself. In the full-length mirror I bought from IKEA to make my bedroom look bigger, in the yellowy hue from the ceiling fixture, I saw my body as it was. No filters. No generous angles. Just the brutal truth of it.

My eyes traversed the flawed landscape until I was too hysterical to keep them open, until my fat, syrupy tears relieved me of the sight.

. . .

I collected compliments in a shoebox under my bed. It started after a strange overnight held by my church when I was fifteen; attendance was mandatory in order to make confirmation. I wasn't particularly religious but figured I owed it to my parents. We were allowed sleeping bags but not sleep. We were kept up all night with prayer and team-building exercises and store-brand snacks. At midnight we received brown paper bags with our names written across the fronts in swirly dark Sharpie. We were told to write everyone kind messages, memories we shared together or traits we admired, and put them into their bag. We were encouraged to sign our names, but it wasn't required, so no one did. We weren't supposed to read our notes until we got home.

I started in the car, despite being deliriously tired and overwhelmed by all the Bible talk. I finished reading them on my bed, knees tucked under my chin, the scraps of paper all around me like snow flurries.

Some were nothing. Fluff. *You're really nice. You're smart.* Others surprised me, telling me I was witty and had a great smile. I decided to save them so I could reread them whenever I was feeling bad about myself. I put them in a shoebox.

Eventually I started adding, writing down sweet things people said to me. Friends. Boyfriends. Professors. Catcallers. I put in pictures, too. Ones where I thought I actually looked pretty or thin. Ticket stubs from movies I liked. Birthday cards from my grandparents. A Post-it with a quote from my therapist about my body being my home, and I should treat it well because it's where I live.

I thought about that quote while on the treadmill, the Goblin turning up the speed from 6 to 6.5. It didn't seem profound anymore. It didn't make me feel good. It felt like a prison sentence.

I decided when I got home, I would pull out the box, read through it.

But when I went to look, I couldn't find it. It wasn't there.

. . .

Dani and I decided to meet up to celebrate a month of our Goblin-ing. We went to a popular salad place for lunch where everyone was content to wait half an hour for a salad and unsweetened ginger lemonade. It seemed like lunacy, but the truth is, a good salad is hard to find.

We ate our salads on a bench in a nearby park. I picked at my spinach, hunting for tiny bits of chicken or tomatoes.

"You didn't get dressing on it?" Dani asked me. "That's commitment. You look amazing by the way. Glowy."

I forked my dry salad. "Has your Goblin stolen anything from you?"

"What? No. Why?"

I shook my head. "Never mind."

"I don't think they're programmed to steal. That'd be, like, crazy."

"I probably just lost it."

"Lost what?"

"Doesn't matter," I said. "Do you have shoes for the wedding yet?"

. . .

Someone told me he had cut his hair. By someone I mean Facebook. I needed another dose of motivation, so I started looking through his pictures, all the way back to the ones with me. Us sitting on a stoop blowing cigarette smoke at the camera. Us in a basement breaking beer bottles against the wall because we were young and delinquent and didn't have to clean it up. Us at a party sitting on a stranger's bed, my legs over his legs, my head on his shoulder, his hands in my hair. Us playing air hockey at a random dive, his arms up in victory and me making a sad-baby face.

I couldn't blame myself. He was beautiful.

The spinach was rough coming up. It was the stems. They got caught.

After, I made myself chamomile tea. It's what I used to do. The smell made me sleepy.

. . .

The group text could not be escaped. An invitation to dinner and drinks from Kelly. Allison couldn't make it Thursday. Friday? I could do Friday, I said. Everyone could do Friday.

What time? Seven? Eight? Nine? Nine was too late for dinner, it was decided. Dani called us grandmas. Is that supposed to be offensive? I asked. I like my grandma very much, Allison said. Same here, Kelly said. Dani said, ha-ha, I guess seven-thirty.

Then came the choosing of the restaurant. Mexican? Sushi? Mexican. Price range? Dos Caminos? Prickly pear margaritas? What about that Latin bistro with the empanadas?

The guava and goat cheese empanadas are the best thing Kelly's ever tasted. Do they take reservations?

I wasn't going. I was never going. Going would mean a guaranteed appearance of the Goblin, and at least two thousand calories. It was one week to the wedding. I was almost out of time.

I bailed an hour before, citing a migraine. I made soup instead.

Kale and chickpea soup.

I was hungry again in twenty minutes. I decided to make toast. Whole wheat.

I left it in the toaster too long and it was dry.

Jam, I thought. A little sugar-free raspberry jam. But I didn't have any jam.

I did have organic coconut spread.

I took it out and started with a thin layer over the toast, burned crumbs flaking off as I ran the knife over it. I took a loud bite. It was terrible.

More spread. I was able to taste the coconut. My mom always said there are two kinds of people in the world: people who like coconut and people who are wrong.

I dipped the knife back into the container.

The Goblin knocked it out of my hand before I could spread it. It hit the floor with a clink-clank-clank.

When I leaned down to pick it up, I heard him say, "Cow."

With that he was gone.

The knife went into the sink and the toast went into the garbage. I sat on my bedroom floor with my laptop balanced on my knees, searching the internet for the best juice cleanse. Edited it to best juice cleanse for weight loss. Organic, cold-pressed. Unpasteurized. Six-day cleanse delivered to my door. Six juices a day. Three hundred seventy-five dollars plus shipping and handling.

I thought if I missed chewing, I could have some celery.

I visualized the way I wanted my body to look, how I wanted other people to see me. How I wanted Ben to see me, or anyone who'd ever overlooked me. To really see me and know that I was beautiful and desirable and that I mattered.

I saw a future where I didn't spend my days obsessing or feeling bad about myself. In that future, I was someone else. Someone who looked nothing like me.

. . .

When I was sixteen a few girls caught me in the bathroom at school and went to the guidance counselor, who turned around and told my parents, along with all of my teachers and my soccer coach. It was a violation of some kind, I was sure, but I was young and meek. It bothered me that everyone knew. It made me feel raw, unsafe.

At the same time, I didn't understand how it was a surprise to anyone. I was a bone. Part of me was hurt that they hadn't said anything sooner, that they hadn't shown any concern.

My mom cried that night; it carried through the walls.

"How could we let this happen?" she asked my dad.

How was he supposed to know what was normal for a teenage girl? He thought I was losing my baby fat. He thought I'd gotten taller. I would never get any taller. Those pencil markings on the wall in the laundry room, there would never be any more. I did damage. I deprived myself.

The vitamin shakes they gave me were foul. I had to pinch my nose to get them down, and as I did, I imagined what they'd look like coming up. Probably the same.

. . .

The day of the wedding, Dani and I sat in traffic eating mushy grapes out of a plastic bag. I skinned each grape with my teeth and then sucked on it to make it last as long as possible. Dani made a playlist of songs we used to listen to in college, and we sang along loudly until all of the songs had played multiple times and the nostalgia wore off.

"Is this going to be weird for you?" she asked me as she searched for replacement tunes.

"God, no," I said, laughing. "Ben and I were together for, like, five minutes."

"Yeah," she said. "Still . . ."

"Ben was always in love with Michelle. It's not like I didn't know. We all knew. I was a placeholder," I said. "I'm glad they ended up together. I'm happy for them."

Dani snorted. "You're either a great liar or a much better person than I am."

I rolled the window down, draped my elbow out of the side of the car, adopting a casual posture. "I'm surprised they invited me."

"You're part of the group. It would have been super shady to single you out."

"I guess."

"Well, you look amazing," she said. "I give up. You pick the music."

I put on a podcast about murder.

. . .

There were violins. There was a sign that read, *Pick a seat, not a side*. There was the added pressure caused by that sign when deciding where to sit, wondering what that seat location could possibly be interpreted to mean. There were the fickle straps of my dress that kept falling, the backless bra that dug into my skin, the shapewear cutting off my circulation.

There was Ben standing at the end of the aisle in an ill-fitting suit. He was too far away for me to get a good look at his face. From where I sat, he could have been anyone. Generic groom.

There was Michelle in her mermaid gown, cathedral veil,

a collection of pretty bridesmaids in not-quite-matching dresses, hair half up, half down.

The ceremony was quick. There were mosquitoes and people crying. There were vows. She promised to be his teammate, but never to keep score. To challenge him, to be patient even when he gets sick, because he's such a baby when he's sick. That got a laugh. He promised to love her always, to put her first, and never to ask her why she needs so many shoes. There was more, but I was too busy willing my stomach to stop howling to pay close attention.

At the cocktail hour, there were drinks named after the couple's cats—Fig and Olive. I sipped tequila slowly, avoided trays of hors d'oeuvres. Bacon-wrapped shrimp and mini quiches and deep-fried mac-'n'-cheese balls.

There were old friends. Todd, Ben's sophomore-year roommate who used to call me Megatron and apparently still did. There was Whitney, a notorious kleptomaniac who once stole Dani's heirloom earrings and then wore them to Dani's birthday party. Now she was a life coach. There was Jenna, who complimented my dress and showed me pictures of her kids. She used to sell weed and shrooms out of a retro lunch box.

There were extended family and an excess of decorative moss and mason jars and tea light candles and a taco bar and a pizza station.

There were table assignments attached with twine to tiny keys.

"What do you think this unlocks?" I asked Dani, holding up my key.

"Probably nothing," she said, not understanding.

There was a highly choreographed entrance of the wedding party featuring props such as fake mustaches and feather boas, followed by the couple's first dance.

That's Ben, I told myself. *That's him.* But he looked so different, clean-shaven, his hair short. And he was having his first dance to "The Scientist" by Coldplay. The Ben I knew would have punctured his eardrums before listening to Coldplay.

"Isn't this a breakup song?" Dani whispered to me.

"Not if you completely ignore the lyrics," I said.

We watched Ben and Michelle sway back and forth, leaning against each other, necks and shoulders limp with exhausted happiness. The burden of joy.

A series of audio malfunctions disrupted the speeches. We could barely hear. I said a quick prayer of thanks to the god of faulty microphones. I downed my champagne.

Salad arrived on gold-and-mint art deco china. Chunks of watermelon and feta and ripe, shiny tomatoes nestled in a bed of romaine. I unfolded my napkin across my lap and reached for my silverware. It was then I noticed my hands were shaking, my fingers spasming, palms sweating.

I was woozy. The only solid food I'd eaten in days was the grapes earlier that morning. I sucked on the lime wedge from my tequila soda but wasn't sure if that counted.

I eventually managed to close a fist around my fork and stab at a piece of watermelon. I deposited it between my lips and let it rest on my tongue. Let it melt there.

"Look who it is."

There was a hand on my shoulder. I didn't need to turn around to know whom it belonged to.

I stood up too fast. For a moment, the room went fuzzy and the floor bounced beneath me. I had to put my hand on my chair to steady myself.

"It's good to see you," Ben said, opening his arms to me.

He wasn't as tall as I remembered.

"Good to see you, too," I said. "Congratulations."

"Thanks," he said. "We're, uh, making the rounds."

"Yep," I said.

"Hey, Dani," he said. "You guys look really good."

"Thank you," Dani said. "We know."

"All right. Michelle went that way, so let me go find my bride," he said. "See you on the dance floor?"

"You know it," Dani said.

"See you on the dance floor?" I said to Dani.

I slid back down into my chair and stared at my salad, anticipating the deep overanalysis of the interaction. I prodded at my emotions with a long stick as if they were something dead in the woods. I interrogated myself. *Are you sad? Are you angry? Are you disappointed? Heartbroken?*

The truth was, all I felt was hunger.

I skewered a tomato. It was only a tomato. Harmless.

But then the next bite, I scooped up a little feta.

I had forgotten the simple pleasure of flavor. I ate the entire thing, fast and frenzied. And my entrée when it arrived. A slab of salmon pink as a sunset resting on top of a fluffy cloud of mashed potatoes, fenced in by soft stalks of asparagus. A golden pool of butter gathered on one side of the plate. I sopped it up with a dinner roll.

"You want mine?" Dani asked, offering me her roll. "I don't want it."

That's when I realized what I'd done. The shame came swiftly. A searing, all-consuming embarrassment.

I couldn't look at her.

"I'm deleting my Goblin," she said. "I'm over it. I'm just not gonna eat bread."

As soon as she said it, as soon as I heard "Goblin," the pain registered. My leg. Ankle. It had bitten me. I looked down and saw it there, fangs dripping blood.

"I have to go," I said. I grabbed my bag and beelined for the bathroom.

It was all marble and neutral pink. Flowers. Baskets of assorted products. Too many mirrors.

I caught a glimpse of myself.

My skin was sallow, my hair damp with sweat. My carefully applied eyeliner was now smudged and uneven. There was a small clump of mashed potato cradled in the silky cowl of my dress. I recoiled in horror.

When I stepped back, I realized it was still there, clamped on me, its tiny jaw hinged around my ankle. I couldn't feel it anymore. I couldn't feel anything, but I could hear it gnawing. I could see the small puncture wounds, the thin streams of blood.

I began to flail, kick my leg, try to buck it off me, but it was clamped on so tightly it wouldn't budge.

"Stop!" I screamed. "Please!"

It occurred to me then that someone could walk in at any moment. I retreated into a stall.

I was panting. All that food. I ate so much food, and it sat in my stomach like cement. My dress felt tight, my shapewear suffocating.

I reached down for the Goblin, but it was on the toilet lifting the seat.

"Do it," it said in that gravelly voice.

When I was done, it flushed for me. Then it stood on the back of the toilet with its arms crossed, looking smug and mean.

"Go away!" I said, wiping my mouth. I was completely exhausted. I sat there on the bathroom floor crying about how tired I was.

"Again," the Goblin said.

I got to my knees, my bare skin cold against the tile, and as I made sure that my dress was shielded from splatter and that my hair was out of the way, I had an image of myself in a wedding dress shuffling around the stall, gathering up an avalanche of white fabric, layer upon layer of lace, and I knew. Even if my life were different, even if this were my wedding day, I would still be alone in the bathroom, hunched over a toilet.

"I can't do this anymore," I said. "I'm done. I'm deleting you."

It snickered. "You can't, stupid. You need me."

"No," I said. "I don't." I stood up. Slid open the latch on the door. As I stepped out of the stall, I heard it growl.

I turned to see it lunging toward me. I leaned back, narrowly avoiding it. It face-planted on the floor.

I sprang forward, smashing my foot down.

I hit the thing. I half expected it to have disappeared, but there it was, stunned, its little legs snapped in different directions, one eye dangling free of its socket. It was hideous.

I crouched down. It made a low moaning noise, and for a moment, I felt sorry for it. Then I saw it smile. A cruel, mocking grin. With both its broken hands, it was flipping me off.

I grabbed it. To hold it was a funny thing; it felt kind of rubbery. It weighed a pound or two. When I squeezed, it had give. Flesh. A pulse. My grip tightened to stop it from thrashing around. A fang scraped the meaty part of my hand.

I always imagined rage to be a red, chaotic state. But it's quiet and translucent and euphoric. A sister to freedom.

I ate the legs first. They were chewy. Once I finished the legs, it stopped screaming. The middle required paper towels. I saved an ear for last. And as I swallowed it down, I realized I quite liked the taste.

BAD DOLLS

I LEFT BOSTON THREE MONTHS after we buried my baby sister. I moved back to the town I grew up in to be closer to my parents and my brother, Bryce.

"You don't have to do this," Bryce said, strategically arranging boxes in the back of the U-Haul. "Mom and Dad are gonna be fine. And I'm around."

"Yeah, well, we're already moving all of my shit, so . . ."

I didn't trust my brother's powers of perception. I knew that my parents were not fine, that he was not fine, that none of us was fine.

We stopped at a Burger King to break up the drive home. We got into a fight in the parking lot when he tried to squeeze the van into a spot that I said was too small, but he was sure he could defy the laws of the physical universe to back into. We weren't speaking.

We ordered separately, paid separately. I was mad because I don't even like Burger King but he was too hungry to hold out for a Wendy's. We sat at parallel tables, each sulking in the same direction. There was a family sitting in the booth across from us. Mom, Dad, brothers, and sisters bickering over small plastic toys.

I didn't have to look at Bryce to know that he was watching the family and that he was crying. He must have known about me, too, because he scooted over and we ate together.

I thought Audrey would have gotten a kick out of that.

. . .

I spent a week in my childhood bedroom fighting a losing battle with insomnia, flipping through old photos at four a.m., listening to my mother cry in her sleep. I realized I couldn't stay there.

I found a place nearby via an ad in the back of the newspaper. I told Jade, my friend and former roommate up in Boston, and she said, "Did you go back to Jersey or back in time?"

"Both?"

I moved into the attic apartment of an old converted Victorian off Main Street, one of the houses I'd been obsessed with as a kid, incessantly pestering my parents about why we didn't live in a house that looked like that. Like a big dollhouse.

It was owned by an elderly lady who wore floral housecoats and walked around with the TV remote glued to her hand. She had thin bluish lips and milky, viscous eyes. She looked like she could die at any moment, leaving behind a bunch of shit she ordered off QVC and stacks of Lifetime movies on VHS. She occupied the first floor. Her grown niece, Louise, and Louise's husband, Jeff, lived on the second and third floors. They had several unsavory bumper stickers on the back of their pickup, empty bottles of Bud Light piled up in recycling. They smoked Marlboro Reds and had bad haircuts. We avoided one another.

The attic was small and cramped, a single room with a sleeping alcove, plus a tiny bathroom with a tub too small to lie down in, a toilet, and a pedestal sink. The kitchen consisted of a counter with a microwave and a hot plate, an adjacent mini fridge. The place had its charm, though, with wainscoting and crown molding, thick planked floors. It worked for me.

I brought my stuff over from my parents' piecemeal. I constructed a makeshift dresser out of cardboard boxes, fearing real furniture would give my subconscious a sense of permanence I refused to grant.

It didn't take me long to discover the doll.

She was in the cabinet built in underneath the window, placed carefully in a silk-lined damask hatbox. She was porcelain. She had shiny green eyes. They looked into mine with unambiguous focus. She wore a sweet blue dress with white lace trim.

"Aren't you just a doll?" I said, thinking I was funny.

I figured she belonged to my landlord. I held on to her for a moment longer, stroking her soft blond hair and thinking of my baby sister, who hadn't been a baby for a long, long time, even though I still thought of her that way. I thought about how when she was a kid, she had never liked to play with dolls. When she was three, she chose to be Maleficent for Halloween over Sleeping Beauty. She chose karate over ballet.

I put the doll back as I found her, thinking I would ask my landlord next time I saw her.

I forgot.

. . .

"Mom, did you want chamomile?" I asked, my voice rising over the scream of the kettle.

"That's fine," she said.

Her mood had improved, but not her appearance. The skin around her eyes was pink, raw from crying, her nose red and scabbed. She blamed herself for my sister's death, and I knew I couldn't convince her otherwise. Bryce had found her a good therapist, and he drove her to the appointments every Monday and Thursday. He acted like a real martyr about it.

I wondered where he had been when Audrey needed him. I bit my tongue. Where had I been? There was plenty of blame to go around. It drifted through the house, moving room to room, a faceless ghost.

Its presence did not go unnoticed.

"It feels heavy in here," my mother said, sipping her tea.

"It's too hot, Mom. The tea." I sat next to her at the table. "What do you mean, it feels heavy?"

"Don't be stupid."

"Do we need to talk to Dad about moving?"

"*We* don't, Mackenzie. I don't want to be a burden to you and your brother."

"You're not. No burden."

"Don't you feel it? Heavy."

"It's hard. Of course it's hard."

"Sometimes I read these stories about people who've had loved ones pass and they'll find something. The person they lost will come back and leave a sign, like a necklace on a pillow, to show they're all right. Audrey hasn't left anything."

"She didn't wear jewelry."

She shot me a look.

I put my feet up on her lap. "I'm sure she's in a better place and will talk to us when we get there."

She pushed my feet off. "You don't believe in God."

"Maybe I do."

She pursed her lips. "Don't patronize me."

"I'm not!" I said. "Jesus Christ."

She laughed and it was the greatest thing to ever happen.

Something I'd been doing and not telling anyone about was going into my sister's room and cleaning and reading her diary. I went through her closet, the one that Mom found her in, and took down all of her clothes and laid them out on the bed. I didn't do anything but stare at them. Then I put them back.

There were certain things in her room I didn't allow myself to touch. Her blankie, her nightstand, her candles, her scented lotions, her hair ties, her books, her snow globe collection—even though the globes used to be mine. My sister was born when I was eight, so a lot of the things in her room used to be mine. Hand-me-downs and knickknacks no longer wanted masqueraded as gifts. I didn't want them back. I just wanted to be among them.

It was weird, I knew, but I gave myself permission because I was grieving.

She would have been mad. It was a violation of privacy, one that transcended death. But whatever. I was mad at her, too.

. . .

One night, after I got back from my parents', I found the hatbox on the floor. I picked it up and opened it.

The doll was bigger than I remembered her, but otherwise looked the same. I put the lid back on and returned her to the cabinet, closed the doors.

"Good night," I said.

I wrote myself a reminder to ask my landlord.

In the morning, when I woke up, the box was on the floor again.

. . .

I got a job at a café down the street, the same one I used to work at when I was in high school. It'd since changed owners and was now called Marlo's instead of Monroe's. It pretty much looked the same: Eccentric portraits of old ladies in feathered hats covered the brightly painted walls; retro furniture cluttered the space. A chandelier made of coffee mugs hung from the ceiling. There was a new espresso machine that had more buttons than I was used to, but I got the hang of it.

"Do you feel like shit working at your old job?" Jade asked me.

"If you mean ashamed, then yes," I said. "But I missed it, to be honest. And if I run into someone from high school and they say something, I can just be like, 'My sister died, so fuck you.'"

"True, true."

Jade was the only friend I still talked to on a regular basis. I planned on getting back in touch with the rest eventually, whenever I could stomach the outpouring of sympathy. They meant well. It wasn't their fault they didn't know what to say or how to say it. Maybe they did. Maybe they were doing everything right and I just wasn't handling it the way I was supposed to. Jade was the only one who didn't treat me differently. I appreciated that.

• • •

There was that middle school field trip to Medieval Times, when I spent my hard-earned babysitting money on one of those princess cone hats with the ribbon. I brought it home and presented it to my sister, expecting eternal gratitude, or at the very least a thank-you and some mild excitement. She provided only disinterest, a sort of "what the hell am I gonna do with this?" reaction that left me bitter.

"Say thank you! Jesus!" my mother huffed from the kitchen, nose deep in one of her crosswords.

"Thank you, Jesus," my sister said, a master of sarcasm at four.

I tried to plan tea parties, play restaurant. I wrote up lunch menus with specials like grilled cheese and pizza bagels, hot dogs cut up in box macaroni.

"What can I get for you today?" I would ask in my best fluffy-waitress voice.

"Cereal."

I could never tell if she was trying to be difficult or if it was embedded in her DNA.

Her rebellion against fashion started at five. She adopted a uniform of black leggings and oversized sweatshirts, both often marked with holes or stains. I took her shopping the day after I got my driver's license and she sat on the dressing room floor wearing an enormous bra on her head instead of trying on any of the things I picked out for her. At the time I was frustrated, asking aloud why I bothered as she giggled at her reflection.

Now I can see that none of it was for her; it was for me.

I was trying to mold her into the sister I wanted her to be, not the one she was. I should have embraced the sister I had, who was reading Stephen King novels in the sixth grade because she appreciated a good scare, who refused to go on the class camping trip because "Fuck that."

She listened to every track of every album on the *Rolling Stone* 100 Greatest Albums of All Time by fourteen, texting me asking if I ever heard of the Doors.

I remember once I was home over winter break and my college boyfriend called to break up with me. I immediately sought out my sister, asleep in her room. I sat at the edge of her bed and woke her up. She yawned, unbothered, asked me what was up. When I told her, her eyes widened and she said, "Asshole!" and I felt better.

She had always been what we called "independent" but now knew was actually "withdrawn." Up in her room, door locked, a do-not-disturb sign lifted from a hotel hanging from the knob. She was on the internet, watching TV, playing video games, reading. Texting. Normal teenage bullshit. Audrey being Audrey.

Whenever I would call or text or try to chat her on Facebook, she was unresponsive. I'd get maybe a few half-baked replies, and thinking she was talking to friends or distracted by homework, I let it go. I stopped trying.

"I'm bored," she complained to me, squished in the backseat of Dad's car on the way to some family function a few years ago.

"Join clubs."

"Don't want to," she'd said.

"I think you're confusing being bored with being lazy."

"I'm not lazy. I just don't feel like doing anything. I don't like doing anything."

"Sounds lazy to me."

"Whatever."

. . .

The doll didn't belong to my landlord. She denied ever seeing it.

"Did someone live here before and leave it?"

"No one lived up there before you, dear," she said. She was always using grandmotherly terms of endearment that sounded condescending. It was how she said them.

"It's not Louise's?"

"I would have remembered," she said. "It's a very lovely doll."

I looked down at the doll. *Lovely.* I thought maybe she could be worth something. I never understood why some people collected things like dolls or Swarovski crystal Mickeys or anything like that, but looking at the doll, it started to make a little more sense.

"Well, thanks anyway," I said.

"You can ask Louise."

"I will," I said, but I was lying.

. . .

"There's a way to tell," my mom said, "if they're worth something. It's the eyes. If the eyes are glass. Are they glass?"

I shrugged. I had used the doll as a conversation starter. I was in the market for things to talk about with my mother. Anything but Audrey.

Typically, I resorted to gossip, a useful tool I believed underutilized by grief counselors and therapists.

I would talk about my cousin Morgan selling makeup over Facebook in what I suspected was some kind of Ponzi scheme, or the weird growth on Uncle Greg's neck that he refused to acknowledge, especially since it had started sprouting hair. I'd talk about the losers my friends dated, about how Katie was snooping on her boyfriend's computer after suspecting him of cheating and found meetup ads he posted on Craigslist under the alias Lucky Todd. He went by James, but apparently James was his middle name. His first name was Todd. He blamed it on his roommate and Katie believed him.

There was Jade's fifty-seven-year-old sugar daddy who had kids her age. Then there was Liz, whose fiancé convinced her she'd contracted chlamydia from a toilet seat.

"People still get chlamydia?" my mom asked.

"Yeah, I guess."

I left out the part about how I'd been seeing a woman before Audrey's death. A tattoo artist from Somerville who had an undercut, a septum piercing, and an anger problem. We broke up before the funeral, when I told her she couldn't come.

There was no point in mentioning it. It didn't matter.

"Your friends are stupid," my mom said.

"No, they aren't."

"They are. If you love like that, you're stupid. But it's a gift to be that stupid."

My parents weren't in love; that wasn't a secret. They got along better now, though.

"You should go hang out with Violet. See some of your old sensible friends."

Violet had been my best friend growing up. She still lived in town. She'd gone to community college and then started a business baking cakes for kids' birthday parties, bar mitzvahs, weddings, corporate retreats, charity events, things like that. She'd also worked part time at the bakery at ShopRite. It was a simple life, one I had thought myself above when I went away to college. I'd judged her for her lack of grand ambition, but I envied her now. I'd never learned to be content with what I had like she did.

We'd kept in touch via liked social media posts, a sweet birthday comment and promise to make a phone date soon. We hadn't actually spoken in years. But she came to the wake. She even cried.

"Yeah, maybe," I said.

"Don't just hang around here for my sake. That won't make me happy."

"I'll call her."

When I got home that night, I considered it. But then I anticipated the higher pitch of her voice, that obvious symptom of sympathy. She'd be surprised I moved home after I swore up and down I never would. I didn't want to deal with it.

I looked at the doll instead.

I tried to figure out what her eyes were made of, if they were glass. I couldn't tell. All I knew was they looked real. So real I could make out the dew in the corners, the dew of active ducts, of the ability to blink without ever actually blinking, to make tears without ever crying.

When I was little, I had dolls that closed their eyes when

you laid them down like they were sleeping. If you never picked them up, they stayed that way. They never woke up.

This doll didn't sleep. She couldn't, not even if you laid her down. Her eyes would never close.

. . .

Chris Mulcahy was a boy I'd dated in high school whom Violet had also dated but in middle school. When you lived in a town as small as ours, it didn't matter. Boys got passed around, borrowed like sweaters. He came into Marlo's looking the way he did when we were together, dark hair disheveled because he woke up late, big blue eyes alert with paranoia like he'd forgotten something but couldn't remember what. All in a way that made him cute and elusive. What *did* he forget? What was he dreaming of that compelled him to continuously press the snooze button? Was it *me*?

"Mackenzie?" he asked like he couldn't believe it, like I was the Easter Bunny.

"Hey," I said. To his credit, it was pretty surreal to be back where I worked in high school, seeing the boy I'd dated in high school who used to visit me and stand in the exact same spot.

"What are you doing back here?" he asked.

"I'm in town for some family shit," I said. "Helping my

parents out for a little while. My sister died. What can I get you?"

"Wow, I'm so sorry," he said. "Wow. I can't believe that. That's crazy. I didn't know."

He wouldn't. He never had Facebook, any of that. I doubted he even had an email address.

"Mocha?" I asked.

"Um, just a coffee. Black."

"Okay. I just put a fresh pot on, so it'll be a few minutes. Is that all right?"

"Yeah, yeah," he said, sitting down at one of the tables across from the counter. "I don't know what to say."

"You don't have to say anything," I said. "Actually, I'd prefer you didn't. Say anything. Not about that anyway. How are you?"

"Uh, me? Um, yeah. I'm fine. Yeah. I'm good. I'm just working with my brother. We have a closet business. Building out custom closets for rich people."

"They need their closets."

"Yeah, ha. They do. They really do. They, uh, have a lot of stuff."

"I'm sure."

"It's good to see you, Mac."

"You, too."

I remembered in that moment how much he had loved me. It wasn't because I was special. He was one of those guys who would marry whoever he was with because that's how he thought it worked. He wrote me notes and drew me stick-figure pictures. We'd hang out in his bedroom and watch his betta fish fight. He'd play guitar and sing funny songs about the kids at our school. I'd kiss his neck and worry he expected more even though he didn't. He was patient with me. We were virgins. We never had sex. I saved that for someone meaner.

Chris always invited me to family events, invitations I declined because I felt too awkward. I barely wanted to be around my own family. He had an older brother, a fireman father, and a mom who worked at the pediatric dentist. She was always ordering "sub sandwiches." I never understood why the "sub" before "sandwiches" was necessary but that's how they said it. It drove me crazy.

His older brother was going to, and eventually did, marry his high school girlfriend. I think his family expected the same of me, trying to include me in their rituals, getting me a Christmas stocking with my name on it and hanging it above the fireplace. It made me deeply uncomfortable. I knew I wasn't going to marry him. And even if I wanted to, I wouldn't have, because he would have asked me to change my name, and I would have had to say no because I refused to be Mackenzie Mulcahy. It sounded like the name of a local politician or a lifestyle vlogger, neither of which I aspired to be.

Sometimes I would get bored at his house and lock myself in his bathroom for long periods of time, cataloging his zit creams and scented body sprays. I told him I had IBS. I don't. I could have come up with another excuse, or just not stayed in the bathroom for so long, but I think I did it to test his love for me. What high school boy would want to hear that from his girlfriend? But he didn't appear put off by it. He saw it as an opportunity to start farting in front of me, which turned out to be the real nail in the coffin. Not the farting; that he expected me to love him enough to accept it.

It was an amicable breakup because he was an amicable guy. A few months later he was dating Jill Marvin and last I checked they were still together.

"Are you still with Jill?"

"Yeah," he said. "Yeah, we got married."

He showed me his ring. I wasn't surprised by it, but I felt something else.

"We should get drinks while I'm in town," I said. "Catch up."

"Yeah, sure," he said. "Yeah."

I handed him his coffee. I told him it was on the house, but I didn't have that power. It would come out of my paycheck.

I called Violet later that day. She had the sympathetic tone I resented but it went away at the mention of Chris.

"Kind of weird he's married to Jill," I said. "The girl he dated right after me."

"Could have been you, Mrs. Mac Mulcahy."

"Jesus."

"You'd be spending your whole life hiding in the bathroom! Eating sub sandwiches."

"Sub sandwiches! I can't believe you remember that."

"I dated him, too, remember? Six months in the seventh grade. In middle school time, that's basically six years."

"I told him we should get drinks."

"What did he say?"

"He said yeah."

"Do you think you will?"

"Who knows?" I said. "We should get drinks. You and me."

"Whenever! You should come over. See my house. I'm always testing new recipes and need feedback."

"Yeah," I said. "I'll come over soon."

• • •

"Mom's therapist wants us to come." Bryce's voice crackled through the receiver.

"Where are you?"

"Driving. Why?"

"Every time you call, it literally sounds like you're calling me from the middle of a tornado."

"The middle of the tornado is the eye, so that's quiet."

"Am I on speaker? It's like you're screaming at me, but I can't even hear you."

"Mom's therapist wants us to come in for a session," he repeated, attempting to annunciate. "Okay?"

"Do we have to?"

"Family session. All of us."

"When?"

"Thursday."

"Can't. Working."

"Our sister is dead, Mac."

"You're an asshole."

I hung up.

As kids, Bryce and I spent a lot of time together because we were so close in age. He was born less than a year after me, my Irish twin. I forced upon him sagas of Barbies and Legos, long epics of backyard make-believe where I was the queen and he was a prince. He always asked to be a knight, but I vetoed it.

"You have to be a prince because I'm the queen and you're my brother," I told him. "Duh."

He dutifully played along.

When we fought, we fought hard. One time I stabbed him in the back with a number two pencil. I think it was by accident during a wrestling session at the top of the stairs, but he claims it went down differently.

I wasn't so selfish. I practiced soccer with him, played goalie, often catching the ball with my face. I let him have the good sled in the winter. We'd trudge down to the ravine, triumphantly taking on the steep slopes, shrieking with glee on the way down, throwing ourselves back up the hill to do it over and over again until our lips turned purple and we retreated inside for hot chocolate.

He was smart but not focused. He would start elaborate projects for the science fair and not finish. The night before, I would sneak downstairs and finish them for him. He never thanked me, but I could tell he was grateful. He even won a couple times.

When Audrey was born, there was a shift in the sibling dynamic. We were distracted by our new baby sister. I liked to dress her up in cute outfits and read her stories; he liked to construct stupid paper hats that made her look like a sailor and draw mustaches on her with nonpermanent marker, something neither my mom nor I found very funny but made my dad laugh like hell.

Bryce never got in trouble, not because he never did anything wrong, but because he was able to fly under the radar. I was dramatic, an attention-seeking overachiever in constant need of validation. Audrey was Audrey. Baby of the family, finicky but favored by default. Bryce got decent grades, played varsity soccer, got scholarships. Now he had a good job as a physical therapist and owned a condo. He was levelheaded and reliable. The ideal brother.

There were times when I felt threatened, like he and Audrey were closer to each other than they were to me. He teased Audrey a lot in that goofy big-brother way. It wasn't cruel; it was a sitcom. He'd come in and she'd tell him to go away. He'd say something obnoxious; she'd roll her eyes. A laugh track would play somewhere off in the distance. I think he missed it, their relationship. He had a void for a sister, but it wasn't one I could fill.

I switched my schedule around at work so I could go to the therapy session. My dad went, too, his discomfort permeating the room and making us all uneasy.

"I think it's important to acknowledge this loss as a family," the therapist said.

Then I stopped paying attention. I mostly just nodded and cried.

We went to Applebee's after, ordered happy-hour appetizers

and a pitcher of beer. My mom and I don't like beer, but we drank it anyway. And a lot more. Peach sangria in fishbowl glasses. Shots of mystery-brand bourbon. We got so drunk we had to take Ubers back to our respective houses.

. . .

It happened before I got the door open. My key was in the lock when I heard it, the pitter-patter of tiny feet, faint music, the twinkly kind, like from a music box. Only I didn't have a music box.

I pushed the door open and caught the doll perched on the edge of my bed, standing upright. When the door closed behind me, she fell onto the floor.

I was dizzy, too drunk to process what I'd just seen. I passed out immediately.

I woke up the next morning nauseous, with a pounding headache. I got up and shuffled into the shower. About halfway through shampooing, I remembered about the doll. The image frightened me: the way she had stood on my bed for that split second looking at me. I remembered the footsteps, the music. I didn't bother to turn the water off. Grabbing a towel, my hair still sudsy, I went to see.

She wasn't at the foot of my bed anymore. She was in her box in the cabinet.

145

I went back into the bathroom, this time locking the door.

I pulled my hair back in a messy bun, left my place, and went to my parents' house to be with my mom, to clean. To occupy myself.

"Remember I was telling you about that doll?" I asked, up to my elbows in dishwater. "Mom?"

She was crying with her head down on the kitchen table. The therapist said it was normal, so I just kept doing the dishes.

• • •

There were still pictures of Audrey in the hall. Her school portraits with that distinct gloss and cheesy laser background. She wasn't smiling with her teeth. She never did for photos. There was no way to capture her essence unless she wasn't paying attention, and even then, if she caught you, she'd force you to delete the evidence.

I liked to remember her best smiling with teeth but there was nothing to help me. I had to rely on memory alone, and that scared me, because memories go. Like everything else, they go.

• • •

Chris texted me first, which was good because I discovered I'd deleted his number.

> Hey Mac good to see you the other day.
> Still down to grab a drink?

I thought about it. Did I really want to hang out with him? Meh. Not particularly. But I did want to get out of my parents' house, where I'd been lingering, avoiding my own place. Avoiding the doll. The memory of it standing on my bed and the mystery of how it got there, it unnerved me. Had I imagined it? Had I taken it out and left it there, forgotten about it? Thoughts of the doll manifested in a persistent chill. It was impossible to get warm, or to close my eyes and not see hers staring back, bright and unblinking.

I needed a distraction.

I told Chris yeah, I'd meet him for a drink. I picked a bar a few towns over where I doubted we'd run in to anyone we knew.

I spent hours getting ready. I chalked it up to boredom but there was probably a dash of desperation mixed in. I wanted to look exceptional. I felt I had something to prove, but I wasn't sure what. Maren, the tattoo artist I'd been seeing, liked me best no makeup, messy haired, natural scented, raw animal magnetism. Which was weird because she was always done up, face painted on, hair styled, lingerie.

I tried not to think about her. When I did, I missed her.

"You look good," Chris said, flagging down the bartender.

"Thanks," I said. "You look the same."

He laughed. "Is that supposed to be mean?"

"No," I said. "Not at all."

He ordered us two whiskeys.

"So, you're married," I said.

"Yeah, yep. About a year. It's cool. It's pretty much the same. Like, the relationship is the same. I guess it kind of changes in a good way. It's hard to explain." He blushed a little.

"I get it."

"You're married?"

"No, I meant, like, I get what you're trying to say," I said. "I'm single."

He nodded.

He told me his parents were doing well. His dad had retired, and his mom had taken up knitting, selling scarves on the internet. His brother and his wife had just had a baby, a daughter they named Spring Angel.

"Really?" I asked.

"Yeah," he said. "Really. That's really her name."

I remembered what it was that had made me fall for him, why I had liked him so much in high school. He was sweet like a ripe peach. Hometown boy. Football on Sundays, help a stranger change a flat tire, adopt a rescue dog and name it Rex, volunteer to coach Little League, collect cans for the food drive. He was good.

And he played guitar.

"I loved you in high school," I said, downing my whiskey. "I did."

He waved the bartender over and ordered us two more.

"I'm telling you so you know. After Audrey, I don't want to leave anything unsaid."

"I loved you, too," he said. "A lot."

"I knew. I mean, I know you did."

He put a hand on the back of his neck and pulled. "I don't think you do."

I cocked my head to the side, a question.

"Nothing," he said quickly. "Just . . . I think I, like, hid how much I liked you because I knew eventually you'd leave."

"Well, I'm back now," I said, sighing.

"You'll leave again. You always wanted, like, more for yourself. That's part of why I liked you so much."

"Thank you." I should have left it there, but he made me feel safe, so I kept talking. "I needed to hear that. Part of me keeps wondering what would have happened if I'd stayed. If I wasn't so obsessed with this idea of leaving, that life was better someplace else. Would I be happier if I had stayed? I could have been there for Audrey. Seen the signs."

"You can't think that way."

"No, I know," I said, something fat and wet in my eye, "but I do. And it's true. If I'd been here, she would still be alive."

"Mac."

I was full-on crying then. "And it's not like my life is so great in Boston. I'm not saving the world. I'm not traveling like I said I would."

"Hey, let's go outside, okay?" He threw cash down on the bar and looked around apologetically. People were staring.

We sat in his car, the same one he'd had senior year, the very car I broke up with him in. He let me rest my face on his chest while I cried. He smelled the same, too. Probably used the same body spray.

I was crying so hard I couldn't catch my breath, but I wasn't crying for Audrey. I was crying for me. For my mistakes, my disappointments, my guilt, my shame. It was excruciating, the guilt. I couldn't live with it and mourn my sister. My brain wasn't letting me. It knew I couldn't handle both. I would die.

I tried to picture the holidays. Christmas, Easter,

Thanksgiving. I couldn't see the empty seat at the table. I couldn't visualize it. I couldn't imagine peeling apples for the pies by myself. Audrey and I had always done it together, making it a competition to see who could peel the fastest. She always won. She didn't know that I let her, that the competition was a ploy to get her to participate.

I was blind to this future without her. The idea of it gave me vertigo.

I kissed him to snap myself back into the present.

He kissed me back.

We were kissing.

Our kisses were hungry. It was the gluttonous kind of kissing that's never enough. I put my hand on his knee, slid it up until I could feel the stitching of his fly, the stiffness underneath. I went for the earlobe, a remembered weakness.

His breath bottomed out. He loved it.

His head went back as I unbuttoned.

"Stop," he said suddenly. "No, no. I can't. I'm married."

"I know," I said.

"That means something to me. I can't. I've never cheated before. Fuck. What do I do?" He turned away from me.

I was agitated. It was better than being depressed but not as good as being fucked. "Well, don't tell her. Let's just pretend this never happened."

"I can't do that."

"Chris," I said. "Please. You felt sorry for me. I was upset. This is familiar. Forgive yourself and move on."

He chewed on his lip as he adjusted himself.

"I didn't just feel sorry for you," he said.

In the years I'd known him, in all the time we'd been together, he had never hurt me until then. He pitied me. I saw it in his face.

"I'm good to drive," I said, opening the car door. I hesitated before closing it. "Don't tell her, okay? It will only cause more problems that no one needs, okay? Forget it."

"Okay, yeah. I will."

"Take care."

"Wait, Mac."

"What?"

"I really did love you."

I didn't say anything else after that. I shut the door.

On the way home I stopped for Chinese food at the place with the best noodles. I got it to go, planning to eat it in bed while watching a dumb movie on my laptop.

I called Jade from the car. "I kissed my married high school boyfriend."

"Liz called off the engagement," she said. "She got another itch and I guess it was the final straw."

"What does that have to do with anything?"

"I don't want you feeling sorry for yourself."

"I'm allowed."

"Not because of that," she said. "Stop making stupid decisions. You're better than that."

"No, I'm not."

"Yeah, you're right."

"Hey!"

"I don't want you to implode. We're getting too old for it to be cute."

"Thanks," I said. "Thank you so much for that."

"You need me to come visit you in Mount Bumblefuck?"

"Nah. I'll be back soon, I think. A few more months."

"You will, Mac. You're not going to get stuck there."

"I know."

"At least you didn't fuck him."

"I would have," I said. "And you're one to talk. Affair with Count Pennypacker."

"What can I say?" she said. "We're a couple of bad dolls."

I told her I had to go. I pulled over to the side of the road to puke out of my car window. It wasn't the whiskey, or the smell of the takeout or the guilt, or the regret over what I'd just done. It was the doll. It was the thought of going home to find the doll standing there, waiting for me. I couldn't bear it. The sense of dread that came over me made me feel small and soft as an egg.

I decided to sleep at my parents' that night.

. . .

I woke up early the next morning and wandered around the house quietly on my toes. I watched TV on mute. I made my parents breakfast, careful not to make any noise with the pans. My dad grabbed his plate of French toast with a mumbled "Thanks," but my mom spent the rest of the day thanking me profusely for being so thoughtful.

"You've always been like this. Ever since you were little," she said. "Always thinking of others."

I made breakfast because I was awake and I was bored. I left the dishes.

I thought about Maren, who had told me all the time how selfish I was, and the night before with Chris.

"Not really," I said.

"You are. Very sweet."

"I mean, sometimes I do nice things but it's mostly for me," I said. "If I'm being honest, I think it's mostly for me."

"Is this that whole 'no selfless good deed' crap? Because I'm not in the mood."

"No, Mom. Never mind."

If I felt guilt over Audrey, I couldn't begin to fathom what she was going through.

"Want to go see a movie or something?" I asked.

"A movie?"

"Yeah."

"Huh. Yes, actually. That sounds fun."

I took her to see some pleasantly formulaic romantic comedy. We stopped at CVS beforehand and bought a bunch of candy: M&Ms and Mike and Ikes and Red Vines. We smuggled them into the theater. We'd been doing this for as long as I could remember, sneaking in candy. A lot of people did it, but it felt sacred to me. A precious secret my mother and I shared.

She seemed upbeat on the drive home, better than she'd been in months, and I wondered if I could be enough for her. If I was enough daughter. Seeing her happy again, I wondered if it was possible for me to shine so brightly I could make her forget about Audrey, make it okay that she wasn't around. This line of thinking coaxed me to say something I knew I shouldn't, curious how my mother would react.

"Sometimes I don't miss her," I said.

"What?"

"Nothing," I said, immediately remorseful. "I don't know why I said that."

"What did you just say?"

"Nothing, Mom. Forget I said anything."

"What's the matter with you?"

"Mom, please."

"Drop me off at home. I don't want you around the house tonight."

"Mom."

"Mackenzie Jeanette. You'd better keep your mouth shut right now, so help me God."

"Fine. Sorry."

I procrastinated going back to my apartment. I went to two different strip malls, stumbling from Marshalls to Old Navy to HomeGoods, looking at useless shit I didn't need and trying to convince myself that I needed it. I left empty-handed.

When I finally got home, I opened the door cautiously. I made noise. I announced my presence.

"I'm home now," I said. "I'm coming inside."

The doll was away in her box, the room quiet and empty. I was by myself.

· · ·

"I kissed Chris," I told Violet as she set down a mug of homemade hot cocoa on the table beside me.

All the furniture in her sunroom was white wicker. There

were American flag pillows, flowers in mason jars, a rooster in the corner, which I worried was taxidermy. The flowers were real. I touched them.

"You did what?" she asked.

"Yeah, I kissed our collective ex. Our married ex."

I could tell Violet because she wasn't judgmental, and she always kept my secrets, no matter how salacious. She was too pure to gossip. A perfect confidante.

She sat down next to me, slurping some whipped cream off her hot chocolate. There were chocolate shavings on top, too. I eyed mine and thought it too pretty to drink.

"How'd it happen?"

"I don't know. We were talking and I got upset about Audrey and then I was crying and then I kissed him. He kissed me back but then he freaked out about it. I told him not to tell Jill."

"Good call."

"You think he will?"

She shook her head. "Probably not. He's not as dumb as he looks."

"Your house is so nice, Vi. I can't believe you live here. It's goals."

"Thank you, thank you! I'm happy with it. It was a lot of work, but I'm happy," she said.

"How's Danny?"

Danny was her longtime boyfriend. He was generic, which was her type. She was a serial monogamist. When it didn't work out with one generic, she'd switch him out for another. I could barely tell the difference. I don't think she could either.

"He's great," she said. "We've been talking about getting married."

"God," I said. "You'll get married in, like, a barn. With all candles. Wine bottles as vases."

She laughed. "Oh, Mac. You know me so well."

"I do."

"And I know you," she said. "It's not a weakness. Asking for help. It's not weak."

I picked up my mug and drank. Too sweet.

"If I need help, I'll ask," I said.

"No, you won't."

I doubled down. "I'm good."

"Okay. But know I'm here if you need me."

"I know," I said. "Thank you."

I took another sip. The sugar went straight up. Instant headache.

"I said something shitty to my mom the other day. I said that sometimes I don't miss Audrey, which was stupid, and

158

I don't know why I said it to her of all people. But it was a lie. I don't think I miss her at all."

I looked over at Violet, waiting for a reaction. Her face was expressionless.

"I mean, I didn't spend that much time with her. I was in Boston for the past seven years. She and I never talked on the phone. We barely texted. I saw her when I came home for holidays and stuff, but there hasn't been a holiday. So, I don't know. I don't miss her. Because it's not real yet. It is, but it isn't. I can't articulate it. Like, I'm sad. But am I sad enough? Should I be struggling to get out of bed? Crying more? My grief kind of comes and goes. I'm not in constant mourning. That's bad, right? I mean, I mostly just feel guilty all the time. Like I fucked up. Like I did something wrong. Like I was a bad sister."

"You weren't a bad sister."

"Yes, I was. I was a bad sister. I was caught up in my own shit. And if she didn't react to something the exact way I wanted her to, I was a bitch. Maybe not directly to her. In general, I was a bitch. I'm a bitch."

"Mac."

"You know it's true. You *know* me."

"You're not a bitch."

"See, you're too nice. That's why we get along so well. We balance each other out."

"I think you need to stop worrying about how you think you're supposed to be dealing with it and just deal with it," she said. "There's no right or wrong way."

I thought about the doll. She'd been on my mind like a blister—a distress I'd gritted my teeth through and tried my best to ignore. I thought about telling Violet. Offering up the doll as proof that there was in fact a wrong way to deal, and that wrong way had a lot to do with a mysterious porcelain doll and my fixation with her. My fear. My suspicion. Maybe then she'd get it, get that there was something very, very wrong with me and how I was handling the loss of my sister.

But I already sounded crazy enough.

Violet tapped her pastel-painted nails against her mug.

I said, "Are you serving me melted chocolate? Is that what this is? Because it's fucking delicious."

She laughed. "Basically."

. . .

I got into the habit of drinking. I would pick up a bottle of bourbon at the liquor store after work and bring it home to my apartment. Drink it squished in the tiny bathtub, legs dangling over the sides, torso soaking in a heap of excessive bubbles, candles burning, wax melting into the tiles. It was indulgent. I felt like I should have been taking quick cold showers instead. But I took baths. And I drank.

I stole a snow globe out of Audrey's room. A small one of New York City, inside it the Statue of Liberty, the Empire State Building, the Twin Towers still standing, flecks of fake snow. I got it on a visit when I was young, too young to remember. I gave it to her when she was too young to remember. I pocketed it during one of my secret trips to her bedroom. I kept it with me. I held a bottle in one hand, the globe in the other, and sat in the bath, waiting to prune up.

I got out when the water cooled, wrapped myself in my thick hotel robe, and put on my fuzziest socks. I sat on my bed reading. There was a rustling over by the window. I assumed the wind. It persisted.

When I brought my eyes up from the book, I saw the doll climbing down from the shelf.

I blinked twice. She landed on the floor with both feet, her black Mary Janes making a faint tapping noise as she began to walk across the floor toward the bathroom.

I stayed perfectly still, paralyzed by shock and awe. I couldn't tell if I was breathing. I was numb, save for a burning sensation at the base of my neck, like someone had struck a match against my spine.

The doll walked into the bathroom. There was a moment

of silence before the door began to creak closed, hinges wailing. It lacked the momentum to latch. A few seconds later, I heard glass breaking.

The doll reappeared, opening the door and pausing there in the doorway to look at me. I thought she might speak.

She began to walk in the direction of her hatbox. When her back was to me, I started to cry, my body's best stab at a reaction to what I was witnessing.

She turned her head, a hundred eighty degrees, back to me.

I bit down on my quivering lip until she turned away and settled back in her box, bringing the lid over the top with her small porcelain hands.

Time passed. Time enough for me to regain control of my limbs, grab my phone, and lock myself in the bathroom to call Bryce.

I almost stepped on a shard of broken glass. The snow globe, which I must have left on the edge of the tub, had been shattered.

"Bryce, I need you to come over now."

"It's midnight."

"Bryce, I'm not fucking around. Get over here now."

"Are you at Mom and Dad's? Is something wrong?"

"I'm at my place. Mom is still mad at me. Just come over. Now. Please?"

"Okay, okay."

I carefully picked up the shards of glass and placed them in the garbage bin. I talked to myself as I did it, repeating, "This isn't real," over and over again until I believed it.

I doubted my sight. I rationalized. I was tired, drunk, stressed, not wearing the glasses I was told I needed in the fourth grade but never got.

It was a creepy doll. It wasn't so far out that my mind would go there.

I thought maybe I had broken the snow globe by accident. Maybe I was having a *Fight Club* moment. Maybe I was the doll.

But then the scratching started. The sudden sound of the latch straining against the pressure on the other side of the door. And the laughing. The giggling. Like a little girl's but not. It wasn't the laugh of a girl.

"Bryce?"

The scratching intensified. I thought the wood was splitting, splintering. Soon. Soon the doll would claw her way inside.

I was nauseous, my heart thumping so violently I swore I could see it through my robe. The edges of the world frayed and then there was nothing.

I woke up to Bryce's pounding. I opened the door to find him red-faced.

"Jesus, Mackenzie. What the hell is wrong with you?"

"Is she out there?"

"What?"

"The doll! Is the doll out there?"

"What doll?"

"You've got to be fucking kidding me."

"Are you going to tell me what's going on or do I have to guess?" he asked. "You've got whiskey breath."

"I'm not drunk. There's a doll. An old doll I found when I moved in here and she's terrorizing me."

He raised his eyebrows.

"Oh, shut up," I said.

"Didn't say anything."

"I know how it sounds, okay? I'm not an idiot. But I swear to God, I'm not making this up."

"I believe that you believe you're being terrorized by a doll."

"Fine," I said. "Can you stay with me while I pack a bag? Can I crash at your place?"

"Where's the doll?"

"On the shelf over there."

He walked over to the shelf. "In this?"

The cabinet was already open. He picked up the hatbox.

"Don't!"

"No?"

"Put it back! I'm serious."

"Why don't we throw it out?"

"It doesn't want me to!" I said, surprising myself. "It'll get mad."

"Ah. Yes. Of course."

We didn't say another word to each other on the way back to his condo. He handed me a blanket and a pillow without a case. He pulled out the couch.

"Night," he said.

He left the light on.

In the morning he made me strong coffee and a Toaster Strudel.

"You have to stop drinking."

"I wasn't drunk. And don't tell Mom."

"Too late," he said. "You have to go to therapy. By yourself."

"Goddamn it!"

"Don't blame me," he said. "What was I supposed to do? You were talking some *Toy Story* shit."

"I'm going to hit you."

"Just don't stab me again. I think I still have lead poisoning. Traces of lead."

"You are so stupid."

"Mom should have put you in therapy after that. You and your pencil shank."

"Exceptionally stupid."

"Sharpening it up with, like, a Swiss Army knife in your room."

"If I had a knife, why would I have needed the pencil?"

"Waiting for the perfect opportunity . . ."

"I'm leaving now."

"Watch out for killer teddy bears."

"Watch out for writing utensils. Prick."

About an hour later, I received the call from my mother.

"Six o'clock tonight. Don't be late."

"Mom."

"Not an option."

"Fine."

"You've always been dramatic."

"What's that supposed to mean?"

"Overactive imagination. When you were five, you were convinced a little boy named Jedediah visited your room at night."

"I have no recollection of that."

"You said he was dressed like a Pilgrim and had black eyes."

"Jesus."

"This will be good for you, Mackenzie. It'll help. I worry about you."

Normally I would have refused but I was grateful to be forgiven after what I'd said to her in the car and didn't want to push my luck.

"I'm going. I'll go."

"Thank you."

I went to therapy. I showed up tired and sloppy, my hair frizzed, mascara smudged. The therapist wasn't fazed. I guess she was used to that sort of thing.

"I'm here because my family thinks I'm crazy," I said. "They thought that before Audrey died, too. So . . ."

"Why do you say that?"

"They've told me. They've said it."

"How does that make you feel?"

"Really?"

"Really."

"It makes me feel like I have a Cassandra complex or something. Like with this doll."

"What doll?"

"This doll that I found in my apartment. It's alive. It moves."

The therapist gave no indication of surprise.

"When did this start?" she asked.

"Shortly after I moved in."

"After moving back? After Audrey's passing?"

"Yes."

"Do you think that you might be associating the doll with your sister? She was much younger than you."

"I don't know. Audrey didn't like dolls."

"You could be projecting some of your feelings about the loss of your sister onto this doll. Do you find it difficult to discuss your sister's death?"

"No, but can we talk about something else?"

"Like the doll?"

"Look, the doll is alive. I don't know what you want me to say."

"The doll is alive?"

"Yes."

"But your sister isn't."

"I'm just here to make my mom feel better," I said. "I'm sorry."

I spent the rest of the session venting about my failed relationship with Maren and avoiding any further discussion of Audrey or the doll.

Though it made logical sense that I would link my younger sister and the doll, I still didn't feel comfortable going back to my apartment. I called Violet.

"I understand not wanting to be alone," she said as she made up her spare bedroom for me.

"Do you have any wine?"

We drank a few glasses lying in the guest bed, playing nostalgia games and painting each other's nails.

"You probably don't believe in it," she said, "but I know a medium. She's a friend of Danny's mom. She read for me once. She's pretty legit."

"Really? Remember that time we played with a Ouija board at Wren Coleman's house, and she got so mad because you kept spelling out 'poop'?"

She snorted into her wineglass. "I forgot about that."

"She was pissed."

"I didn't believe in any of that until Sadie. She told me things she couldn't have known. Things I never told Danny. Like, she knew my grandfather flew planes in the war and that my grandmother used to bake fresh bread whenever I would go over there as a kid. She said she died of lung cancer and kept touching her throat. It was pretty crazy."

I had a vision of the medium telling me something about Audrey, like that she was somewhere happy and safe. That she didn't blame me or Mom or anyone. I could tell her that I loved her and that I was sorry. Promise to stop touching her stuff. Even if it was a sham, I thought it would be nice.

I thought maybe it'd make the doll stop moving.

"Okay," I said. "Set it up."

. . .

The weather started to change. Summer slouched into autumn, the trees exposing their skeletons, leaves shriveling at their feet.

Violet turned the medium thing into a whole ordeal. She baked. Cupcakes, brownies. She served fresh ground coffee and hot apple cider with cinnamon sticks and set out a vegetable tray. She made dip. A casserole. She invited three other friends: two who had recently lost parents to cancer, the other apparently just curious and morbid. The air in her house was warm and silky from countless linen-scented candles.

The other friends cornered me, asked me questions. They touched my hands like they knew me. I would rather have been back at my apartment with the doll.

Not really, though.

I hadn't slept at my apartment in almost three weeks. Not since the night with the broken snow globe. I returned only during the day to get new clothes or grab a forgotten charger. I kept the door propped open and stayed on the phone the entire time. Always with Jade.

"Stop calling me in the middle of the day," she'd said. "I have a job."

"I need you."

"Okay, okay. I'm here."

I slept at Violet's or Bryce's or my parents'. I continued to lift stuff from my sister's room. Used school notebooks, stuffed animals. I stashed them in my old bedroom, bottom-left drawer of the dresser. In high school I had hidden condoms there.

I asked Violet if I could have my reading last and she said I could, but then one of the other girls started crying before her turn, so I went instead.

It was cold in the dining room. Sadie, the medium, looked like your average soccer mom with slightly better hair. She wore a turtleneck.

"Hello," she said. She sat at the head of the table. I sat a seat away, not wanting to get too close.

She reached out for my hand. She had to stand up and hunch over the table.

"I can just, like, move over," I said.

She smiled and nodded. She took a deep, hearty inhale.

"Who is Alex?" she asked.

I shrugged. "No idea."

"There's an Alex coming through for you," she said, her voice buttery, sweet.

"I don't know any Alex," I said. "Boy or girl?"

"Male. A strong male presence. Alex."

"Nope."

She was undeterred. "He says you've always liked his smile."

"Presumptuous."

"He says he will see you later." Sadie inhaled again. "You are very lost."

I laughed.

"I'm seeing a spotlight. You want to be an actress."

"No," I said.

"Light. You need light. You search for light. Spotlight. Fame."

"I don't want to be famous," I said. A lie. I wanted to be a little famous. Everyone does.

"I'm getting a Judy. Judy is coming through. Judy is here with us in this room."

"Okay."

"She says hello, darling. Judy."

"Nope. Don't know any Judy," I said, starting to get antsy. I was eyeing the clock, calculating how much time I had left with the medium. She did only fifteen minutes. Any more than that she claimed was too taxing.

I realized then that the reading was a terrible idea.

"No Judy," I said. "Sure the name is Judy?"

"Yes, Judy, darling. She says you don't know her."

"Oh, does she, now?"

"Judy. Judy has a message for you."

"It's not Audrey, is it? Not Judy. Audrey?"

"Judy. It's Judy. Judy says—" Sadie's face went white. She slammed her hands down on the table so hard I jumped. "Judy says the doll is not Audrey."

"What?"

"The doll isn't Audrey. It's not Audrey. Mackenzie, darling, the doll is not Audrey. It's not Audrey."

I was choking, the air robbed from my throat.

"The doll is bad. The doll is bad. The doll is bad. The doll is bad. The doll is bad. The doll is bad."

"Okay!" I stood up fast, the chair falling behind me. "I get it!"

Sadie shook her head. "I'm sorry."

"Did Violet tell you something?" I asked before remembering I never mentioned the doll to Violet. "Do you know Bryce? Is this a joke?"

"I'm sorry. I don't choose the messages that come through."

"Come through where? I don't know any Judy. I don't know any Alex."

Violet poked her head in. "Everything okay?"

"No," I said. "This isn't funny. I don't know a Judy. I don't know an Alex. I'm not darling. I came here to talk to Audrey. Aud-rey. That's who I came to talk to. I want to talk to Audrey."

"All right, come on, Mac. Let's get you some cider," Violet said. I saw her mouth, *Sorry,* to Sadie.

"Don't apologize to her," I said. "She's messing with me. She's a fraud. I don't know anyone named Alex. I don't know a Judy. Who the fuck is Judy?"

"Mac, calm down."

"I'm not going to calm down. This is bullshit. My sister is dead and I'm talking to Judy? Who's Judy? Where's Audrey? Huh, lady? Where's Audrey? Where's my sister? When's she coming through? Where's Audrey?"

It was a scene. The whole house was silent except for the sound of me screaming my sister's name.

"And how did you know about the doll? How did you know about the goddamn doll?"

Sadie looked solemn, sad for me.

"Answer me. Tell me," I said. "Was this a joke? Tell me the truth. Please?"

"I'm sorry," she said.

"Jesus Christ! Are you serious right now?"

She went pale again. "You have to get rid of the doll. The doll is bad. It's not her. You have to get away from the doll."

"Oh, thank you. Thank you so much. My sister is dead. Do you even give a shit? Do any of you give a shit?"

"Mac," Violet whispered.

"You know what? Have fun with your grief brownies, cunts."

I slid a casserole dish off the counter on my way out.

I went home to play with my doll.

• • •

The memories came back swift and ruthless. The time we got ice cream sundaes for dinner, just she and I, sitting in the back booth at Friendly's, tying cherry stems into knots with our tongues and harassing the waitress for sides of hot fudge. The time in Florida on our family vacation when I took her to the pool after dark and we played Marco Polo. We walked back to the hotel on our tiptoes, sidestepping lizards on the pathways, keeping an eye out for loose change for the vending machines. We shared a bed that trip and she stole all the covers. I remember her warmth, how loud she snored, the weight of her on the mattress. Her prickly knees against my back as she tossed and turned.

"Hold still," I hissed, but she slept through it.

I remembered the pictures she used to draw when she was little, the stories she wrote. Someone always died in her stories and I thought it was because that's what happened in Disney movies. Someone died. I didn't think about it as real life. But it is. People are always dying here, too.

I wondered how the world must have looked to Audrey, how bleak. I scraped the bottom of myself for whatever hopelessness I had, scrounging for the darkness that I thought might bring me closer to her state of mind. I wanted to gather enough to understand. But there wasn't enough of it for me to know.

And there wasn't enough of anything to keep her here. Mom wasn't enough. Dad wasn't. Not Bryce. Not me.

Not enough.

· · ·

The doll was already in my bed. I climbed in beside her and petted her hair. It was yellow the way Audrey's had been when she was a baby. When she was first born, I used to sing to her in her bassinet as she slept. "What a Wonderful World." "Can't Take My Eyes Off You."

"Silly, huh?" I asked the doll.

No answer.

Sometime after that, I fell asleep.

. . .

I dreamed of her future. Sitting at the kitchen counter filling out college applications. Sending me pictures of prom dress options, asking my opinion. She was going on alternative spring break with friends from her dorm, building houses in Iowa. She was out at a bar, with me, freshly twenty-one and drinking mojitos. She was graduating, her cap crooked, gown enormous because she didn't order the right size. She got her first job, a new car, an apartment with hardwood floors and a dishwasher. She was in love, and it turned her green eyes neon with happiness.

. . .

Bryce's nose was an inch from my nose. "Holy shit!" he kept saying. "Holy shit."

"What is it?"

"What did you do, Mac? What did you do?"

"What?"

I felt a vague sensation running up and down my skin. I rubbed my eyes and sat up, and the sheets fell away. I found myself covered in scratches. I experienced a few moments of confusion followed by singular, horrifying clarity.

"What did you do to yourself?" Bryce asked me.

"It was the *doll*."

I jumped out of bed and ran over to the bathroom mirror. My face was scratched to shit. My neck was bleeding. I reached my arms overhead and felt more scratches on my back, sharp divots in my skin, razor-thin.

Bryce was pacing. "What the hell, Mac? Violet said you had a meltdown. What's going on with you?"

"The doll," I said. It hurt me. It *hated* me.

"Not this again," he said. "You have to stop with that doll, Mac. We're getting rid of it. Setting it on fire. I don't give a shit."

He returned with the hatbox in his hands. He lifted the lid. He shuddered when he saw it.

"What?"

"Nothing," he said. "We're having a bonfire tonight. I'm taking this."

"Careful, Bryce. Be careful with it."

"Sure," he said. "We'll do it at my place. Don't let Mom and Dad see you like this."

I was busy examining my scratches.

"Mac? Don't let Mom and Dad see you."

"Duh."

"Get yourself together, all right? I can't be worrying about you right now. Understand?"

178

"I didn't do this!"

"Do you hear what I'm saying?"

"I hear you."

After he left, I cracked a window and let the cool air in. A sense of safety descended in the space. I sat on the floor, tracing the red lines along my body and contemplating the sad, strange turn my life had taken.

If I lived in a world where dolls could come alive, couldn't I live in a world where I could travel back in time to save her? A world where I could bring Audrey back from the dead? I considered the rules of reality, how easily they seemed to bend and break.

I thought I might say a prayer. I thought I might put my faith in something. I thought I might take my mom to church.

I slept instead.

. . .

Bryce opened two bottles of beer. He handed me one, motioned for me to sit down beside him on the back steps.

"Remember when we told Audrey we had a brother named Adam who was born before her and we kept him locked in the shed?" he asked.

"No."

"We told her he was disturbed, so we kept him in Dad's shed. You really don't remember?"

"Should we feel bad?"

"I don't know."

"Did you ever think something was seriously wrong? With Audrey, I mean."

"No," he said. "It was school. She was lonely or whatever. She never had a ton of friends. I mean, she had some friends. But yeah. I don't know. It was in her head. It wasn't us."

"You sure about that?"

He shrugged, then chugged the rest of his beer. "Let's light this bitch up."

He started the fire. He had a nice pit, the kind they sell at Bed Bath & Beyond. Meant for toasting marshmallows, not demonic dolls. He got the hatbox from inside.

"You know, you might be right," he said. "This thing might be evil."

"Did something happen?"

He didn't respond.

The air smelled of lighter fluid. When I closed my eyes, I envisioned the box in the snapping blue flames. I saw ashes that weren't ashes, that would never be ashes.

I was overcome with the sense that what we were about to do was wrong. That burning the doll wouldn't destroy it.

That whatever malevolent force possessed it would just find another vessel. I had no explanation as to why I felt this way. Maybe I'd seen too many horror movies. Maybe I'd just lost my mind.

"Stop," I yelled. "We shouldn't burn it!"

"What? Why?"

"What if it isn't a doll? What if it's, like, a spirit or a demon living *inside* the doll? And if we burn the doll, it finds a new host or takes another form."

Bryce looked at me a minute. "Okay. You're officially crazy."

"Bryce, please."

"Mac."

"Please! Listen to me."

"I am. I'm not gonna burn it."

"Thank you."

"Sure."

We stayed quiet for a long time until the fire died. He said he'd hang on to the doll until I decided what I wanted to do with it. He walked me out to my car, hugged me. We hadn't hugged since we were children. It was awkward but nice and it made me cry. He was my whole history, my brother. My future, my partner in crime.

I spent the night with my face in my laptop, Googling

things like possessed doll drop-off and evil doll disposal and Kübler-Ross. I discovered my stage and, after an extensive search, a paranormal expert in New Hope, Pennsylvania, who went by the name Ms. Mercury.

> Dear Ms. Mercury: I'm having a problem with a doll that I found in my apartment. I think it's evil. I don't know where it came from. Is this the kind of thing you handle? Sorry if not.

She wrote back the next morning saying, Sorry to hear. Yes, I will take the doll. Please let me know when you will be by.

I got Bryce to drive out there with me the next day.

"I can't believe I called out of work for this," he said.

"I'll buy you Burger King."

He stayed in the car while I went to drop off the doll. He offered to take it for me, but I wanted to do it. It needed to be me.

Ms. Mercury lived in an old Colonial painted electric blue. There were gnomes along the pathway engaged in various gardening tasks; there was a sign that read, *Don't feed the faeries*. I kept looking over my shoulder at Bryce's car in the driveway, grateful he was there and that I hadn't come alone. The doorbell chimed like a cuckoo clock.

She looked as expected. Long silvery hair, an excess of jewelry.

"Come in," she said.

I could smell incense burning. A hint of cat piss. "No, thanks," I said.

"Come," she insisted, taking my wrist. She pulled me in before I could wriggle away.

Her house was somehow scarier than I had anticipated. The foyer was covered floor to ceiling in dated wallpaper and sepia-toned portraits of people frowning. She led me to a home office, completely generic aside from a corner sectioned off by a velvet curtain.

"Sit," she said, drawing back the curtain to reveal a small round table and two metal folding chairs. There was a stack of frayed tarot cards on the table. It occurred to me then that this was the second mystic I'd sought out in the past week. I was instantly nauseous.

I put the hatbox on the table and pushed it toward her.

"You're smart to get rid of it," she said, shuffling the tarot cards. "It's already quite attached to you."

"Attached?"

She reached over and touched the scratches on my face. I turned away.

"I have a charm for you," she said. She set the cards down

and disappeared behind the curtain, returning moments later with a dyed rabbit's foot on a beaded key chain.

"Keep this with you at all times." She resumed shuffling, then spread the cards in a half-moon in front of me.

"Pick," she said.

"I don't want a reading, thanks. I just want to drop off the doll."

She tucked her hair behind her ears and, with a shrug, folded the cards back into a tall, neat pile.

I stood up, ready to leave and put it all behind me. But I couldn't help myself. I had to ask, "What will you do with it?"

"I have a trunk for such items. I'll keep it locked in there for now," she said. "I have a contact, a specialist in these cases. Very experienced with dolls. You're welcome back to meet him. He's quite handsome."

"Thanks," I said, "but I live far."

She tapped her bottom lip. "Okay, then, darling. That will be two hundred seventy-five."

"Sorry?" I had heard her perfectly clearly. I just couldn't fucking believe it.

"Twenty-five for the charm, and two fifty for the doll."

"You're charging me?"

She looked at me like I was insane. "Of course. I'm providing a service."

"I didn't realize," I said. "I don't have cash on me."

"Quite all right. I take credit."

I wondered if the trauma of the doll outweighed my disdain for bullshit. It didn't.

"Never mind," I said. I put the rabbit's foot on the table and picked up the hatbox.

"Never mind?"

"I'll deal with it. I'll take it. Thanks for your time."

"I don't recommend you leave with that doll. It's very, very dangerous."

"Thanks," I said, breaking into a light jog. I saw myself out. I didn't exhale until I was back in the car.

"What took so long?" Bryce asked. "What happened?"

I shook my head. "Just drive."

I opened the lid of the hatbox.

"It's still in there?" he asked, almost running over a garden gnome while backing out of the driveway.

"She wanted three hundred bucks."

"Christ!" he said. "What are you gonna do with it now?"

I thought about it for a minute. I rolled down the window for some air, hoping the wind on my face would help me figure things out. Maybe I should have paid the money. I worried I had just passed up my only opportunity to be rid of the doll.

But then I realized maybe I didn't want to be rid of her.

Maybe I liked the distraction. Maybe I liked the abuse. Maybe I liked *her*. Yes, she hated me, but her hatred was something I could understand. I hated me, too.

We got each other. We were bonded. Attached.

I decided I wasn't ready to let her go just yet.

I rolled up the window. "I'll come up with something."

"You can't keep that thing," he said. "Mac?"

"I don't want Burger King. Let's get pizza."

. . .

Later, we ate greasy slices of pizza on the living room floor, using our laps as napkins. Mom, Dad, Bryce, and me. We called it drive-in style but really it was just lazy.

Mom picked off her pepperoni and gave it to Dad. Bryce left his crusts for me. I left mine for Audrey.

"I'm not even going to ask what happened to your face," my mom said. "Jesus, Mary, and Joseph."

Bryce cleared his throat.

"I fell," I said.

"You've always been a little uncoordinated," she said. She suddenly started laughing. It got my dad going. Whenever she laughed, he laughed.

"Remember that time . . ." Her voice trailed off; she was laughing too hard to finish.

. . .

I went into Audrey's room after Bryce left and my parents were asleep. I put everything I'd taken back in its rightful place.

"I'm sorry," I said.

I lay down on her bed and closed my eyes.

A vague amount of time passed before I recognized I wasn't alone.

I could feel someone there. A presence, a warmth. Weight on the mattress. Breath on the back of my neck.

I knew when I turned over I would find either the doll or my sister.

I waited a long time before I looked.

ACKNOWLEDGMENTS

Thank you to Lucy Carson for embracing these stories, for believing in them, and for finding them a home. To Heather Carr and Marin Takikawa for their early reads and perceptive notes.

Thank you to Amble Johnson, Jai Punjabi, and Steph Kent for their notes and encouragement on "Reply Hazy" and "Bachelorette." To One Story and the talented writers at the Summer Writers' Conference who workshopped "Goblin." To Halimah Marcus and Electric Literature's Recommended Reading for first publishing "Goblin."

Thank you to Jessica Wade for her continued faith and always insightful edits. To Laura Wilson and the entire team at Penguin Random House Audio and at Berkley—I'm grateful for your hard work, and humbled by your talent.

To everyone who helped bring Jordan, Nat, Meg, and Mackenzie to life, thank you.

ABOUT THE AUTHOR

Rachel Harrison is the author of *Such Sharp Teeth*, *Cackle*, and *The Return*, which was nominated for a Bram Stoker Award for Superior Achievement in a First Novel. Her short fiction has appeared in Guernica, in Electric Literature's Recommended Reading, and as an Audible Original. She lives in Western New York with her husband and their cat/overlord.

Connect Online:
Rachel-Harrison.com
Instagram/TikTok: RachelHarrisonsGhost
Twitter: RachFaceLogic

For more fantastic fiction, author events,
exclusive excerpts, competitions, limited editions and more

VISIT OUR WEBSITE
titanbooks.com

LIKE US ON FACEBOOK
facebook.com/titanbooks

FOLLOW US ON TWITTER AND INSTAGRAM
@TitanBooks

EMAIL US
readerfeedback@titanemail.com